The Struggle for Kathy's Soul

MW01248363

Copyright © 2024 by Karen Ross

ISBN: 978-1-77883-501-8 (Paperback)

All rights reserved. No part of this publication may be reproduced, distributed, or transmitted in any form or by any means, including photocopying, recording, or other electronic or mechanical methods, without the prior written permission of the publisher, except in the case brief quotations embodied in critical reviews and other noncommercial uses permitted by copyright law.

The views expressed in this book are solely those of the author and do not necessarily reflect the views of the publisher, and the publisher hereby disclaims any responsibility for them. Some names and identifying details in this book have been changed to protect the privacy of individuals.

BOOKSIDE Press

BookSide Press
877-741-8091
www.booksidepress.com
orders@booksidepress.com

Contents

Acknowledgments

I WISH TO THANK THE MANY people who helped and encouraged me along the way. Much appreciation goes to Bonnie Kearns, Anne Croskey, Carol Levin, Marsha Moran and Jamie Hill for their time and suggestions. To Linda Alkana and Phyllis Rosenhalf for their valuable help with the editing. And a very special thanks to my sister, Kathy Wyse, for her constant support and for being my biggest fan. This book would not have been possible without Kathy Kricensky, who I will remember always.

Preface

I WALKED INTO WORK THAT DAY totally unaware of the news that waited for me inside. I was a therapist in a family service agency that served children. I didn't particularly care for my supervisor. She was a tall woman, about fifty, with thinning bleached blond hair. She always looked very professional in her tailored suits and matching high heels, in contrast to the rest of the staff, who dressed in jeans and sweat shirts. She tried her best to be friendly, but it didn't seem real to me. To me she seemed like a very cold, hard woman.

But that day, when she came into my office, she seemed different, almost compassionate as she asked, "Have you heard from Kathy lately?"

I thought it was a strange question. I knew she had met Kathy years ago, but had no idea that she was in touch with her recently. I tried to sound casual as I answered, not wanting to reveal that I still thought of Kathy every day. "No. I haven't talked to her in more than six months."

She looked at me sadly. "I thought you'd want to know. She died yesterday."

CHAPTER ONE

I WILL ALWAYS REMEMBER THE FIRST time I saw her. It was September 2, 1975. I had just gotten my master's degree in social work two months earlier and was interviewing for jobs. I was feeling pretty desperate and discouraged since the job market back then was very competitive. I had been on about fifteen interviews already and hadn't even received one call back. This particular day I had an appointment with the director of an adoption and foster care agency. We had finished the interview and stepped out of his office. As we walked down the hallway, he paused by an open door. Inside were two women unpacking and stacking things on shelves. One of them was very preoccupied with what she was doing and didn't look up from her task. The other woman was casually dressed in blue jeans and tee shirt. She looked up and gave me a friendly smile. "Hi. I'm Kathy Adams," she said as she walked over to shake my hand. Her hand was as warm as her eyes. I liked her instantly.

The director led me into another office and informed me that the supervisor of the foster care program would be in shortly. I felt that I had made a good impression on him and was frustrated that I'd have to do it over again with someone else. I hated these interviews. I hated all the questions. By now I knew all the right answers, but I felt they were looking for more. If I didn't get a job in social work soon, I'd probably have to get a job as a secretary somewhere. Just the idea of it turned my stomach. But I was running out of money. I was hoping this supervisor wouldn't judge me harshly because I'd just gotten out of school. I was trying hard not to be negative, but my confidence was at a low.

When the door opened and Kathy walked in, I nodded and smiled. I assumed she was a clerical worker. When she said "I'm sorry to keep you waiting", I was shocked. The surprise must have shown on my face because she started to chuckle. "I know you weren't expecting me. We're real casual around here on the days we don't have clients. I hope you're not disappointed." Disappointed! No Way! For the first time, I felt hopeful that I had a real chance to land a job. I felt an instant connection with her.

She told me about the position and then asked the usual questions -- where did I work before, what type of therapy did I have experience with, what types of clients did I like to work with? I answered as honestly as I could, but I started getting nervous again. I wanted more than anything to make a good impression. She sensed my insecurity.

"It's really difficult finding a job these days, isn't it?"

"It's been so discouraging. Everyone wants counselors with years of experience. The competition is really rough."

"I'd rather hire a new graduate. That way I can train someone the way I want to. I have to approve it with Dave but he made it clear that if I wanted to hire you, I could. So, I have the final word. When can you start?" I was thrilled! I wanted to kiss her!

We agreed that I would start the following Monday. She held out her hand as we said goodbye.

"Thank you so much," I said, knowing I would be grateful to this woman forever.

"You might not thank me when you find out how hard I'm going to work you," she joked.

"You won't be sorry. I'll do a really good job for you."

"I know. I'm not the least bit worried." I knew that she meant it.

I couldn't wait to get home to tell my roommate. Lynn and I had been living together since our second year at Ohio State. I met her the first day of classes. We just said hello but a month later I went to a party and she was there alone. We hit it off right away. She was from New York, having come to Ohio State to get away from her family. She joked about her typical Jewish upbringing, and, since I was also Jewish, she felt a real bond with me. I think that we were the only Jewish women in the whole program.

We became good friends quickly and spent a lot of time together over the next two years. We were both athletic and loved playing tennis and softball. And she loved going to the movies as much as I did. We went every Sunday afternoon. We were even sexually involved a few times but it was more of an experiment for her. She was really into men. For a while, I was jealous of the guys she went out with, but I liked her so much as a friend, I got over it. I didn't want to lose her because of jealousy. It never would have gone anywhere anyway.

About two months before we were going to graduate, she asked if she could come to California with me. "I just can't go back home. We wouldn't have to live together, but I'd want us to stay close."

"Of course, we'll live together!" I was thrilled. It had always been difficult for me to make new friends and I had been dreading the day I'd have to say goodbye.

After graduation, we packed everything into her car and took off. She had never been west of Ohio, so we stopped at all the tourist spots along the way -- the badlands of North Dakota, Mount Rushmore, Yellowstone, Reno, Lake Tahoe, and Yosemite. When we finally got to Los Angeles, we were exhausted. It took a few days to find an apartment, but we discovered a great little community right near the ocean called Seal Beach.

She found a job almost immediately, while I was still pounding the pavement.

I stopped at the store and bought the ingredients to make a great dinner. After all, I had something terrific to celebrate. I had the table all set and everything cooked by the time Lynn got home.

"What's up?" she asked walking through the door. "We're celebrating!"

"You got the job!" She threw her arms open, gave me a big hug, and kissed me briefly on the lips.

"Tell me all about it." I tried to remember every detail, but I didn't mention Kathy. From the very beginning, my life with her was private.

CHAPTER TWO

I CAN'T REMEMBER IF IT HAPPENED all at once, or slowly, over time. But at some point in my past, my self became separate from my feelings. It had more to do with my mother than my father. She was the emotional center of our family.

I grew up in Cleveland, Ohio. There's an old joke about Cleveland. It's a great place to leave. There were three of us. My brother, Joe, was two years older; my sister, Annie, was two years younger. That made me the middle child. I think what they say about middle children is true. The oldest child gets the parent's undivided attention, at least until the second child is born. The youngest is the baby. The middle child doesn't really have a role. Joe was my mother's favorite. Annie, my father's. That left me out. But in a strange way, it made things easier for me. I couldn't disappoint them as much as Joe or Annie could. They didn't notice me as much.

Oddly enough, this didn't upset me on a daily basis. But every once in a while, I remember standing in front of our medicine cabinet in the bathroom with a bottle of pills in my hand thinking, "They'll be sorry if I die. I'll make them sorry." I don't remember specifically what happened to drive me to the bathroom. I just remember the feelings -- jealousy, envy, anger, and hurt.

My father was a nice-looking man with thick, wavy brown hair that was graying at the temples. He was short, with a stocky frame. He didn't talk much, but he was a powerful presence in our home. The one thing I remember most about him was that he rarely smiled. I guess he didn't have much to smile about.

He worked two jobs to support our family and was gone from 6:00 in the morning until 8:00 at night. Even though he was gone most of the time, I never questioned that he was in charge. When he was home, there was always a lot of tension. I remember being a little nervous and afraid. We would all be on our best behavior. If we weren't, he'd get angry. Mom would use this to try to keep us in line. I can't count the number of times she'd say, "Wait until your father gets home." She would never follow through though; she didn't have the heart to turn us in.

Annie was the only one who would greet my father at the door when he came home. She'd give him a big hug. She wasn't afraid of him at all. But then Annie never did anything wrong.

The only meal he ate with our family was on Sunday. It was the only meal all week that not one word was spoken. He barely talked to anyone, except to give an order. He always seemed so angry. I used to wonder what mom talked to him about in the privacy of their bedroom.

Even now, I still feel sad that he wasn't more affectionate with me. I always hoped he would change. I don't remember ever sitting on his lap, or having him read me a story or even giving me a piggyback ride. He never said, "I love you." He never took us to play in the park. Besides providing for us financially, he wasn't much of a parent.

Looking back, I don't think he was a malicious person. I just don't think he knew how hurt I felt when he ignored me. I never told him. I didn't know how. I would just pretend I didn't notice. When I think of him now, I refer to him as Julian. It's hard for me to even say the word father or dad or daddy. He was a stranger to me.

My mother was a different story. How I loved her! Through the years she sacrificed so much for all of her children. We always came first. When we were young, all three of us thought she was the most wonderful person in the world.

She was pretty, with a pixie haircut and beautiful olive skin. She was smart too. And she was very vulnerable and caring. We always knew how she felt about things. I remember feeling so much joy when she was happy. She had a wonderful smile. She loved to play with us. Everything that was lacking with my father, was made up tenfold with my mother.

She would always say her greatest joy was being with her kids. She made us feel as if we were the most important people on earth. She gave each one of us a wonderful gift---her unconditional love. Even though she showed Joe more attention, she had plenty of love left over for Annie and me. When one of us complained that she loved Joe more, she would explain that when Annie and I were babies, Joe didn't get much attention. She had to make up for that now. She was always so sincere that it was hard not to forgive her.

Both of my parents were Jewish, but not religious. My maternal grandmother was the only one in our family that really followed Jewish traditions. She would have big family dinners on the holidays. On Passover, we would all read passages from special prayer books. I hated Passover. I was the only kid who would stumble over the words. Mom would have to help me. I could see my younger cousins snickering. Mom would come to my rescue with a big hug or a kiss and a "That was great, sweetheart." What a great lady!

But mom had a dark side too. Sometimes she would cry so much that I never thought she would stop. We all tried very hard not to do anything that would upset her. She seemed so fragile when she cried. It just broke my heart when I made her unhappy. The guilt would be unbearable. Looking back with my knowledge as a social worker, I can see that she had problems with depression long before we even suspected that something was wrong.

Sometimes my father would make her cry. Late at night, I would hear him talking to her in an angry tone of voice. He was usually upset with her because he thought she was too easy on us. He was probably right, but I hated him for making her unhappy. Then I would wish that he'd go away and never come back. I thought that our home was so much happier when he wasn't there.

When my father was at work, the four of us had a wonderful time together. I cherish those memories now -- even more so because of what happened later. My favorite time of day was at dinner. Mom would cook every night. We had a booth in our kitchen, like they have in restaurants, and we'd sit around and tell each other about our day. We each had a turn. Mom would hang on to every word.

Joe tried to be funny. He would play practical jokes on Annie and me, like putting salt in our milk or taking our dessert when we weren't looking. I would get mad, but mom would laugh. It was hard to stay angry when mom laughed. Joe was always better than Annie or me at making her laugh. That was the thing I liked best about him. Unfortunately, he lacked other good qualities. He was handsome and very popular and started having girlfriends when he was nine or ten. Mom told him he was too young, but Joe didn't listen. He started babysitting Annie and me when he was twelve. One night he taught us how to play strip poker. When we were all naked, he got Annie to feel his penis. I told mom about it when she got home. It was the first time I ever remember seeing her angry with Joe. It was a silent victory for me. But it really never changed her feelings about him. He was still her favorite. However, she never let him babysit us again.

Annie was a really shy child. It was always my job to watch out for her. Annie didn't have a mean bone in her body. I used to take advantage of that as much as I could. If mom gave me a chore to do, I'd pass it on to Annie.

She never minded. She was much better at chores than I was. The only time mom ever got angry with me was when she saw me picking on Annie. Then I would feel terribly guilty and be extra nice to Annie for a few days. We had a pecking order in our home that never changed.

Joe would pick on me, then I would pick on Annie. Poor Annie. She never had anyone to pick on.

Besides mom, Annie was my best friend. We played together from morning until night and, most of the time she went along with anything I wanted to do. Annie and I shared a room. We'd lie in bed and talk for hours before we fell asleep. Our favorite topic was movie stars. She loved Tony Curtis. My favorite was Robert Wagner. I remember arguing with her about who was cuter. I don't think we ever resolved it. Mom let us hang pictures of our favorite stars all over our room and on Saturdays she would take us to the movies. I'll never forget how frightened I was of the witch in "The Wizard of Oz" or the joy of my first musical, "Singing in the Rain."

Even though he didn't seem like an important part of our lives, everything changed when my father suddenly died. He had a massive heart attack on his way to work one morning. Mom was alone when she got the call. She waited for all of us to come home from school so that she could tell us together.

She didn't cry when she said it. "Your father died this morning." For the longest time, I thought that I killed him. After all, I had wished many times that he wouldn't come home. I didn't tell mom because I thought she would hate me for what I did. So, I just kept my guilt feelings inside. My grandparents took us to their house while mom made arrangements for the funeral. Annie cried for two days and though I tried to comfort her, I wasn't much help. I tried to understand her sadness, but I just didn't feel the same way. After all, I wasn't his favorite.

It was a very beautiful funeral. I was surprised that so many people were there. The casket was open. I was afraid to look inside at first, but I knew that mom wanted me to say goodbye to him. As I walked toward him, my legs were shaking, my throat was dry and my eyes were burning. I was shocked when I looked inside the casket. The undertaker had made his face look strange and slicked down his hair. It barely even looked like him. He looked hollow inside. When I leaned over to kiss him goodbye, it hit me. This was my father! And I was never going to see him again! "Daddy! Daddy!" I cried. I don't know where that voice came from. It didn't sound like me. But now that he was dead, I lost all hope of ever getting the affection I always wanted from him. And I was sadder than I had ever been in my life.

I felt mom's arms around me. "It's Ok, Susie. Daddy will always be in your heart. He'll always be with us."

At the end of the service, the rabbi pinned black ribbons on us and cut them down the middle. Grandma explained it was to show that we were mourning a family member. We all had to "sit shiva", an old Jewish tradition that included sitting on uncomfortable stools for seven days. Everyone who came to visit brought food and sat with mom on the stools and said wonderful things about my father. I felt very guilty. I couldn't think of anything wonderful to say.

I heard mom crying in her room every night. I would go in and pat her back. "It's okay, mommy. We'll take care of you. Please don't cry." How I hated to see her cry!

And then, one day, a few months later, she stopped. I was thrilled. I was going to get my mother back. But she wasn't the same. She tried. She tried very hard. But the joy was gone from her eyes. It broke my heart.

She started working at my grandfather's hardware store to support our family. That left us kids to fend for ourselves. By this time, Joe was thirteen, I was eleven, and Annie was nine. Mom divided the chores evenly, but Joe was becoming quite a bully and made Annie and me do most of his chores too. We didn't tell mom. She was so tired when she came home that she could barely hold her head up. We didn't want to burden her more than she already was.

Annie and I would make simple things for dinner, like hot dogs and hamburgers and tuna salad. On weekends, mom would make something special and take us to the movies. Joe was playing baseball on the Junior High School team and was busy practicing. So, Annie and I had mom for ourselves. We were on our best behavior and never complained about all of our chores when most of our friends were "carefree". As I look back, I can see that we just wanted to protect her from any more pain. Just as I never told my father how I felt, now I started hiding my feelings from my mother. I never told her how much I missed and longed for our old life.

By the time I got into high school, both of my grandparents had passed away. They were such a great support to all of us, especially for mom. When things got too hard for her, they would have us over for a few days so that mom could get some rest. My grandmother would cook all of our favorite foods. She spoiled us almost as much as mom did in the old days. They left mom the money my grandfather got when he sold his hardware store, so things were a little easier financially. She had a new job as a bookkeeper for a dry-cleaning business. The owner's son took a liking to her. She began coming home late. One night she didn't come home at all. Annie and I were frantic. We called everyone she knew, but no one had seen her. Joe called the local hospitals. She finally showed up at about 5:00 AM. When I heard her at the door, I ran to open it. She was kissing a man. My mom! How could she! I was furious. I slammed the door, tears streaming down my face. She was angry when she followed me in. "What's wrong with you, Susan? I didn't raise you to be rude." I think I knew that something significant was happening but I couldn't put it into words. The days of mom putting her kids first were over. Mom had discovered that she was attractive to men.

I don't remember how I learned about sex. I just knew you weren't supposed to talk about it. At least we never did at our house. On my first real date, when I was fifteen, I went to the movies with a boy that was two years older than I was. When the movie started and the lights went out, he put his arm around me and lightly touched my breast.

It felt good, but I instinctively pushed his hand away. I felt angry that he did it. I didn't even know him! I never told anyone about it. I was too embarrassed. I didn't go out with a boy again for a long time. I felt more comfortable with my girlfriends.

But mom went out with a lot of different men. She didn't say anything, but I knew she was having sex. She seemed very happy for a few years, but I didn't like this happiness. I was very jealous that her happiness wasn't connected to us anymore. It was like she had a secret life that didn't include us. I had a secret place in the basement where I would go sometimes. I'd go there to cry when the feelings of loneliness were unbearable. How I missed her! I didn't want Joe or Annie to know about it. They seemed happy for mom. I didn't want them to know that I was so selfish. I couldn't sleep when mom wasn't there. So I'd go to my private place and cry. I felt so frightened that one day she wouldn't come home. And she'd be gone forever. I was frightened that she didn't love us anymore.

When I was seventeen, I got a part-time job after school doing office work. My boss was the most handsome man I had ever seen, except in the movies. He was very tall, with dark hair and a dreamy smile. I thought he looked like Rock Hudson. He was the first adult I met who didn't treat me like a child. He always said please when he gave me an assignment and thank you when I finished it. He had a way of looking at me that made me feel very important. I hadn't felt that way in a long time. He was married with two children. I knew nothing would ever happen between us, but he was really my first love. I was just crazy about him.

When Annie and I were invited to go on a vacation with close family friends for two weeks, Mr. Davis asked if I knew someone who could fill in for me while I was gone. I was relieved when mom said that she'd do it. I was afraid someone else might try to steal my job from me. How I wish it were only my job that was stolen.

When we got home and I got back to work, Mr. Davis seemed glad to see me. He started driving me home after work and would stop in to say hi to mom. I could tell that she liked him too. After he left, I'd go on and on about how wonderful he was. One day, mom got angry and told me she thought I should quit my job. She thought I was getting too attached to him. I was furious. "You're just jealous," I shouted. "You're jealous that he likes me better than he likes you!"

I ran down to the basement screaming, "I hate you. I hate you." If I knew what was really going on at that point, it would have saved me a lot of heartache.

We didn't talk about it again. I kept my job, but Mr. Davis stopped driving me home. By then, mom had gotten her own phone. She'd be in her room for hours talking about it. We'd hear her laughing and giggling. Annie said she was happy for her. Joe was gone most of the time and didn't care what mom did anymore. It felt like I was the only one that was lonely and miserable. It felt like we didn't really have a family anymore.

One day I came home from school early. I had a bad cold and just wanted to sleep. I froze when I saw Mr. Davis' car in the driveway. I opened the door slowly, hesitantly, afraid of what I might find. But there wasn't anyone in the living room. I walked up the stairs. Mom's door was closed. I knew what was on the other side, but I had to see for myself. When I opened the door, mom screamed. I just remember standing there, staring at them. Mom tried to cover Mr. Davis with the sheet. Then she started to cry. I didn't say anything. I just closed the door softly behind me. When I went to the basement, I didn't cry. I felt stupid. And I felt betrayed. I didn't know who I hated more. Unconsciously I started banging my head against the wall. I think I wanted to feel the pain I was in. But I couldn't. When I finally came upstairs, Mr. Davis had left. Mom was in a robe getting dinner together. "Susie..." I wouldn't listen. I pushed past her out the door. I walked for miles. On my way back, I saw Annie. "Susie, we've been so worried. Are you okay? What happened?" I didn't tell her the truth. I guess in a way, I was still protecting mom.

I quit my job the next day. I never saw Mr. Davis again. I knew mom still saw him, but he never came to our home anymore. She tried to make it up to me. She stayed home more in the evening and took Annie and me to the movies again. We went once a week. At least something good came out of it! One night, I heard her crying in her room. I went in and sat next to her. "Oh Susie, I'm so sorry. Can you ever forgive me?" I hugged her close and for a few minutes, it felt like I might really get my mom back. My heart was filled with joy.

Then she told me that Mr. Davis might leave his wife so they could get married. I didn't let her see me cry. I held it in until I could get to the basement. By then, I was very good at hiding my feelings.

Mom didn't marry Mr. Davis. Instead, his wife found out about the affair and threatened that if he didn't end it, she'd take him for every penny he had. I don't think he ever intended to marry mom, but I never told her what I thought. Mom was so crushed! I wanted to show some sympathy towards her, but I couldn't. When I heard her crying in her room, I didn't go in to try to comfort her anymore. But Annie did. It became her job now. I don't know if mom ever noticed. She never said anything about it. Not sharing our feelings had become a pattern in our family.

After Mr. Davis ended their affair, mom didn't go out with other men. I think she was really in love with him. I could understand that. It was the one thing that mom and I still had in common. Those were really dark days for her. She couldn't seem to snap out of it like she had in the past. It was even worse when Joe went away to college. They hadn't been close in years, but he was still mom's favorite. Annie would try to cheer her up by taking her shopping or out to dinner. Mom tried to put up a good front but we both knew how unhappy she was. We just didn't know what to do about it.

Annie found her the first time she attempted suicide. She was lying in the bathroom with an empty bottle of pills nearby. Annie called the police right away. They saved her life. She spent the next two months in a psychiatric hospital. I was horrified the first time I went to see her. She was in the locked ward. When two aides brought her out, I could tell that she was heavily medicated. She had dark circles under her eyes with a blank stare. She didn't even seem to recognize Annie or me. She didn't have makeup on and her face was very pale. Her clothes were wrinkled and disheveled, with runs in both of her stockings. We both hugged her but her body was limp and she didn't hug us back. She didn't say a word the whole time we were there. "My mom. I want my mom. Please come back," was all that kept going through my mind. Both Annie and I were devastated.

The doctor told us that she had a serious mental illness called Schizophrenia. I know now that the doctor was an idiot. She didn't have Schizophrenia. She was in a Major Depression. But back then, I didn't know about mental illness and just trusted what the doctor said. They put her on medications that caused awful side effects. It was supposed to quiet down her thoughts so that she wouldn't get so upset. In reality, I think it killed a lot of brain cells and stopped her from thinking all together. The doctor assured us that the medication was keeping her from suffering. I prayed that was true. I never wanted her to suffer.

Things at home went back to the way they were after dad died. Annie and I took care of running the house. But this time, we had to take care of mom too. She couldn't work anymore. Her brain worked too slowly on the medication. Most of the time she just stared at the television. It was an awful time for all three of us.

I went to work as a secretary, while Annie stayed home to take care of mom. She had to be hospitalized three more times the next year. She didn't attempt suicide outright, but there were times when we couldn't get her to eat or leave her bed. Though Annie and I begged him to come home to see her, Joe never came, not even once. I hated him for that. I think it scared him to know that he had a mentally ill mother. He just didn't want to deal with it.

After the fourth hospitalization, Annie decided to take mom on a trip to the Grand Canyon. She thought it would cheer her up. When we were younger, mom always talked about all of us going there. Mom actually looked excited before they left. I hugged them both goodbye and helped mom into the car. When she was comfortable, I stooped down beside her. I took her hand in mine and whispered, "I forgive you, mommy. I love you."

She looked at me and just for a moment there seemed to be some life back in her eyes. She lifted my hand to her mouth and kissed it. "I love you too, Susie. I love you too." I had a lump in my throat as they drove off, but I didn't cry. I think I was afraid if I started, I would never stop.

I got the call two days later. It was from a police officer in Colorado. "Is this Susan Kramer? I hate to tell you this, Miss Kramer, but there's been a car accident. Your sister, Annie, and your mother were killed earlier this morning." That was the final blow. I didn't feel anything.

Joe came home for the funeral. I looked at the two coffins in front of me with no emotion. I was just as dead on the inside as mom and Annie were. Joe didn't stay for the week of "sitting shiva." So I sat by myself on the stool and greeted the people that brought food and talked about how wonderful mom and Annie were. I didn't see Joe after that. I could never forgive him for not visiting mom the whole time she was ill. She had sacrificed so much for him and he gave nothing in return. I just added him to the list of men that had disappointed me.

I left Cleveland shortly after that and never went back. There was just too much pain there. It was no surprise to me when I decided to go into social work. If I couldn't deal with my own pain, at least maybe I could help others with theirs.

Some people believe that there are no accidents in life. Everything happens for a reason. When I walked into Children's Home that day, I was desperate for a job. I would have taken anything. I never would have guessed the impact the job and Kathy would have on my life.

Until I met her, I never understood how the power of love can heal.

CHAPTER THREE

I FELT NERVOUS DRIVING UP TO the building, partly because I wasn't used to all of the traffic on the busy California freeways and partly because I suddenly realized I was actually going to have to use the skills I learned in graduate school. I was sure I forgot everything. The site was located in a sleazy part of Long Beach. The buildings were old and run down. Graffiti was scribbled everywhere. The sidewalks were littered with paper and garbage. A few homeless people were pushing grocery carts loaded with old clothes and cans they collected to turn in for money. I was a little hesitant to get out of my car. After I walked in, I was greeted by one of the clerical staff and led to a large office with several desks. Mine was in the back. I was introduced to Helen, Steve, and Mindy who were the adoption specialists. They had been at Children's Home for several years. Mindy was the most attractive of the group and also the friendliest. She took me on a short tour of the building. I recognized Kathy's office, so I stuck my head in and said hi. She smiled and motioned for me to come in. Because I was so nervous in the interview, I hadn't noticed that her walls were covered with colorful posters. Beautiful. emerald green plants lined the windows. I paused to take everything in.

"How do you get your plants to look so healthy? Mine always die in a month, tops."

"Yeah, everyone comments on them. I guess I just have a green thumb. I inherited it from my mother. Our house was always full of plants and flowers. Sit down." I sat in the chair next to her and waited.

She was looking down at the papers on her desk and began to sort them. I just watched her. She was truly lovely, with brown, shoulder-length hair that fell softly around her neck. Her skin was very white and smooth. But her eyes were the most striking part of her --very round and deep and blue. When she picked her head up and looked at me, it took my breath away! I found it difficult to concentrate on what she was saying.

"You're going to be running the older children's foster care program. So, the first thing you have to do is recruit the foster parents. We have a list of people to call for interviews.

I'll go with you to the first one so I can show you how to do it. After we have enough parents, then we'll be able to start placing the children."

I must have looked overwhelmed because she stopped and smiled.

"I know it's scary at first. I've been there. I think you'll do great". She seemed so insightful. I learned very quickly that it was difficult to hide my feelings from her.

"Thanks. I need all the encouragement I can get." "So, how did you get interested in social work?"

"When I was about seventeen, I was having some problems at home. Teenage stuff. So, I saw a counselor a few times and she really helped me. I never forgot it. And you?"

"I guess it was pretty similar for me. I never went to counseling, but I did spend many summers at camp. I admired the counselors I met there. Since then, I've always wanted to work with children. This job is a dream come true for me. You know, Susan, we've interviewed a lot of people for your position. Dave kept saying I was being too picky. But I was determined to hold out for exactly the right person. I felt very strongly about you right away. You just seemed so honest and sincere."

"Wow, that's really a wonderful compliment. Thank you."

"These kids we're going to work with have been through so much." They've been deserted by their parents, for God's sake! I just have a strong feeling that you can identify with that. I think I'm a good judge of character and you strike me as a very caring, vulnerable, and loyal person. I think the kids will connect easily with you. I know that I did."

"That's a lot to live up to." I hoped I wouldn't disappoint her. "I think you know how much it means to me that you're giving me this chance. Between you and me, I'm going to work my ass off!"

"Well then, I guess you better get started."

I think I was actually glowing as I walked out of her office.

I followed her around for the next few days. We did a home visit with a potential foster couple and she let me sit in on several of her counseling appointments with some of the parents that were placing their kids. I admired the ease with which she got people to open up about very private, personal aspects of their lives. She was so warm and supportive. And she really listened to people. She was the first person I truly admired and wanted to emulate. She was very patient and kind to me and consistently made herself available. I loved the time I spent with her. I often told her how terrific I thought she was and how lucky I felt that I had such a wonderful teacher. It surprised me that I was so open about my admiration of her. It wasn't like me to let my guard down.

We both worked late one night and walked out of the building together. When I turned on the ignition, my car wouldn't start. I had to go back in the building and call Lynn to pick me up. "I'll wait with you," she yelled.

We were laughing and talking together when Lynn showed up. I introduced them and they briefly said hello before Lynn and I drove off.

"So that's why you've been coming home in such a good mood. She's really pretty. Is she gay?"

I laughed. "Can't I ever hide anything from you? No, she's not gay and nothing is going on. She's just been very kind to me."

"Right!" she said sarcastically. I just ignored her.

When I saw Kathy the next day, she commented, "Your roommate seems nice."

"She is."

"She's not just your roommate, is she?" It shocked me that she was so direct.

"No, she's not." She was silent. "How do you feel about that?"

"What you do outside of work is really none of my business," she said coolly.

I couldn't help wondering then, why she brought it up. "I'd like it to be. I mean I'd like to be open about it. I mean I'd like us to be friends."

Her face softened. "I'd like that too. But right now, I'm your boss and we have work to do."

CHAPTER FOUR

THE NEXT FEW WEEKS WE were very busy getting the program together. Kathy did a lot of work at home. Every morning, she came in with notes and charts. She didn't seem to have much of a social life.

One night I stayed late with paperwork. I walked past Kathy's office on my way out.

Her door was closed, but I heard her crying inside. I called out, "Kathy, are you OK?" When she didn't answer, I walked in. She was sitting at her desk with her head down and hadn't heard me come in.

"Kathy," I said again as I touched her shoulder.

She was startled and jumped. She looked at me with red eyes and a tear-stained face.

Then she put both of her arms around my waist and buried her face just below my breasts and started to cry again. I didn't say anything. I just put my arms around her and held her. The last time I had comforted anyone in such an intimate way was years ago with my mother. It was wonderful to be that close to her but it also felt scary and awkward. When she stopped, she pulled away and reached for a tissue. I could tell she was embarrassed. She didn't look at me when she said, "Thanks, Susan. I really needed that."

"Do you want to talk about it?" I said quietly. "I'd like to help if I can." "You already have. Anyway, I'm just having a blue day and feeling sorry
for myself. Don't you ever have them?"

I thought about my mother's "blue days." Those days that turned into weeks and months.

"I feel sad sometimes, but I don't let it out very often."

"Sometimes this job is so draining that I just feel overwhelmed and exhausted."

"Come on. Let's go someplace and get some coffee." "That sounds good."

When we got to the diner, we grabbed a booth in the back. "Do you live alone?" I asked.

"I live with my brother. We came out here at the same time, so we decided to buy a house together. I think he gets tired of listening to me. I can get pretty intense sometimes.

"I love that about you. You can be intense with me anytime," I said jokingly. I was sorry that I said it. It felt like I was flirting with her.

She looked surprised. "I might actually take you up on that."

We sat together silently for the next few minutes. Kathy had her head down, stirring her coffee as if she needed something to do. I felt like I had made her feel uncomfortable. I just watched her, not knowing if I should share my feelings. I decided not to. I didn't want to scare her away.

When she looked up, she smiled and started talking about work again. "How would you like to do a group together."

"I'd love it. But you'd have to help me since I've never done one before." "I haven't either, but I love doing new things, don't you?"

I hesitated. "I'm not sure. I don't think I'm as courageous as you are." "Are you kidding? You're one of the most courageous people I know." She surprised me. "Why would you think that?"

"It's pretty brave in this day and age to have an open relationship with a woman."

I laughed. "Well, it's not very open. Look. I didn't mean to mislead you. Lynn and I were involved in the past, but we're not lovers now. She's not gay, just curious. When you asked about her, it just seemed like an easy way to tell you about me. But you already knew that." I paused. "Does anyone else in the office know?"

"I haven't said anything, if that's what you're asking, and I haven't heard any gossip about you," she said with a smile.

"Good. I'd like to keep it that way."

"I can understand that. A lot of people still feel very negative about it. I think it's probably a very difficult life style."

"Yeah. I had to find that out the hard way. Last year I finally got up the nerve to tell my best childhood friend. She was shocked. She said it didn't matter to her, but she hasn't called me since. I've called her a few times, but she makes up excuses to hang up quickly. It's been hard on me. I haven't told anyone else since, until you. I can't see myself really being out."

"I'll bet you would if you met someone that made it worth it for you." "Maybe. What about you? Have you ever been in love?"

"I'm not sure. I thought I was once -- in High School. We went out for several months, but he was looking for someone more attractive. It broke my heart. Then in college, I had a boyfriend for three years. He was a wonderful man. I considered marrying him for a long time. But in the end, I just wasn't in love with him and it wasn't fair to go on for either one of us. So we broke up."

"The guy in high school sounds like a real jerk. I'll bet he never found anyone that even compares to you."

"You're really good for my ego, Susan. I think I'll keep you around."

"Why don't we do something together this weekend? It will be good for you to get your mind off of work. There's a new health club that just opened up near my condo.

Let's check it out. We can get massages."

"Sounds good." She paused. "I have to get going. This has been great. We'll have to do it more often." She gave me a warm hug and squeezed my hand.

I thought about her all the way home. I was aware that the physical attraction I had for her was getting stronger every day. It frightened me. I didn't want anything to upset our working relationship. But it also excited me. It had been a long time since I felt attracted to anyone. I had almost forgotten how wonderful it could feel.

On Saturday, we met outside the club and walked in together. I had been there a few times before and was actually thinking of joining. Kathy's eyes were wide as she looked around. It wasn't very crowded but there were several muscular, good-looking young men lifting weights. She watched for a minute, then turned to me. "I guess that's not your thing, huh." I laughed. I liked it when she teased me.

The attendant led us to a dressing room. We both just stood there for a minute. I knew she was just as uncomfortable undressing in front of me as I was in front of her, so I said, "I'll wait outside until you're in the massage room."

"Thanks," she said gratefully. She didn't look at me.

The massage was incredible. My masseuse was very skilled in using just the right amount of pressure to relax me. Her hands seemed to glide over my body, pausing at the parts that needed the most attention, like my neck and shoulders. When she was finished, she wrapped a big towel around me and led me to the sauna. As I lay down on one of the benches, the door opened. I didn't look up. I knew it was Kathy. She stood at the door for a moment before walking in. "That was perfect," she said softly as she sat down near me. I forced myself to sit up, but kept my eyes closed. I didn't want to look at her just then. I was too nervous.

She was quiet for a while. Then she asked, "Was Lynn your first lover?" I knew she meant woman.

"No. I had a few experiences before but they were very brief." "How old were you?"

"It was after I was married. My husband and I were both twenty-two. I was a virgin and he was pretty inexperienced sexually. Our wedding night was a disaster and it never got much better. When I look back on it now, I don't think it was entirely my fault. He was a real slam bam thank you ma'am kind of guy, if you know what I mean. The marriage only lasted eleven months."

"I've had a few of those myself. So, you've been married?" "Yeah."

"You're full of surprises."

"Anyway, for a long time, I thought there was something wrong with me because I never had a climax. After we divorced, I went out with lots of different guys and found out there wasn't. In fact, I really liked sex with men, if they took their time. I discovered that I was quite orgasmic. What was missing for me was the emotional closeness I had with some of my girlfriends." She was totally silent, so I continued.

"When I was about twenty-five, I was working for an insurance company and sat in a room typing policies with four or five other women. It was very boring so there was a high turnover. One day, this very attractive woman was hired and my boss asked me if I would train her. She was married, but as I got to know her better, she confided in me that her husband didn't satisfy her sexually. He had gained a lot of weight and didn't have much of a libido anymore. We got to be good friends. I had a boyfriend at the time, so we started double-dating. The guys really liked each other too. They had a lot in common. So, while they watched sports together on TV, Judy and I were usually off somewhere together, shopping or just talking in their bedroom. I really liked her a lot. I think she knew that I was attracted to her and she would flirt with me, but she always stopped short of any physical contact.

"One Friday night we decided to drive to Las Vegas for the weekend. Her husband drove and Rick, my boyfriend, sat with him in the front seat. Judy and I were in the back. I don't know if you've ever driven to Vegas at night, but between Barstow and Vegas, there are no lights. It's pitch black.

"Suddenly, I felt her hand on my breast. I was shocked, but I didn't move away. Then she said, 'Are you tired? Why don't you lie down? You can put your head on my lap.' When I did, she covered me with her coat. Then she proceeded to feel me up the entire way to Vegas, with her husband in the front seat. It was the most exciting, erotic thing I've ever done."

I opened my eyes. I was smiling as I turned to finally look at her. "I haven't thought about that in a long time."

"What happened to her?"

"We drifted apart. We lost contact after I left the job a couple of months later."

"I mean, were you ever with her again?"

"A few times. She finally left her husband about a month later and stayed with me for a few days. We stopped short of actually making love, but there was a lot of kissing and petting going on. Then she started dating men and that was the end of me." I laughed again, but Kathy was very serious.

"That sounds painful."

"I was devastated at the time. But I have never regretted the experience. I'd do it again in a minute."

CHAPTER FIVE

WE WERE SITTING IN HER car at McDonalds, having a quick lunch and talking about the program. When we were finished, she hesitated a moment. "I have to talk to you about something and I really don't know how to begin." She looked away.

"You look so serious, what is it?" I was beginning to pick up on her body language when something was bothering her.

"About three years ago I was involved in a lawsuit and the attorney that took my case was a young, attractive lesbian. I was hesitant to hire her at first, probably because I've always been so uptight about that issue, but I went ahead and did it anyway. And in the process, I found myself very drawn to her and attracted to her in a sexual way. I never told her about it because it scared me to death and I've tried to get it out of my mind and not think about it. But every once in a while, I have a dream about her and I wonder what would have happened if I had expressed my feelings." She was looking straight ahead the whole time she talked, but now she turned to face me. There were tears in her eyes. "And now, it's happening again, with you. I could dismiss it once, but a second time?" She shook her head. "I just can't deny it to myself anymore." She took my hand and rubbed it softly in hers. Then she put it up to her lips and kissed it. "I'm just so confused and scared. But I couldn't hold it in any longer."

I couldn't believe this was happening. After months and months of wishing I could be with her romantically, I was paralyzed to do or say anything. I wanted to tell her that I was scared too and that I didn't want to get hurt. It was okay to love her in silence, but now it was out in the open. Could I, would I take a chance on her?

We sat in silence for a long time. I didn't pull my hand away and she didn't let it go. Finally I said, "It's okay Kathy. I'm not going to take advantage of you or rush you into anything you're not ready for. I know what you're feeling. I've been there." I gave her hand a supportive squeeze. "I remember the first time I felt sexually attracted to a woman. I was nineteen. I was on a date with my current boyfriend. We were bowling with some of his fraternity friends and their dates. One of the girls was very attractive. She was dressed in sexy, tight jeans and a low cut blouse. Every time she bent down to throw the ball, I couldn't take my eyes off of her ass. Talk about being scared to death!"

Kathy laughed, but was quickly serious again. "I don't just want to look at you. I want to hold you and, and...I don't know what else really. I just want to be close. It's practically all I think about." She let go of my hand with one last squeeze and we drove silently back to the office. All the way back, I wanted to tell her how I felt about her, but I still couldn't. It just was too soon. When we got to the building, she turned the ignition off quickly. I grabbed her hand as she was pulling out her keys. "Kathy, I want you to know that first and foremost, I'm your friend. You can talk to me about anything. I think you're an amazing woman. You're one of the warmest, most open, insightful and beautiful women I have ever met."

Her eyes teared up again. "In a way I already regret what I've told you. I know it will change everything between us. You can pretend it won't, but it will." With that she pulled out her keys and got out of the car.

We didn't speak again for the rest of the day. She was right, of course. Things would change. Our relationship just took a turn I never expected, but secretly longed for. And the only thought I had over and over was "Please God, don't let me fuck it up."

She took the next few days off. I was worried about her and missed her terribly but resisted the urge to call. "You're not avoiding me, are you?" I kidded when she returned. She looked tired. Dark circles were beginning to appear under her eyes. They didn't sparkle like they usually did.

She looked up at me, hesitantly and tried to smile. "I'm not sure," she answered honestly. I would come to learn that no matter how painful, she was always honest. "I keep remembering my best girlfriend when I was about seven or eight. She was very affectionate with me. One day my father saw her kiss me on the cheek. He asked her to leave and forbid me from having her over again. He told me it's not normal for girls to kiss each other and ordered me to stay away from her. I was dumbfounded and confused, but I never questioned my father. I felt awful that he acted that way to my friend and I was embarrassed when I saw her at school. We barely talked anymore. But I kept hoping that my father still loved me after I had done such a terrible thing." Her eyes filled with tears.

"It will be okay, Kathy," I said. It was hard to see her in such turmoil. "There's a big difference between feelings and behavior. You haven't done anything wrong." She didn't respond.

After a minute I said, "Maybe you should talk to someone." "I have...the minister at my church."

"And?"

"He told me to pray and live by God's word."

Oh brother, I thought. You can't be serious! "Uh huh, I guess you're in big trouble." I tried joking with her. She finally laughed.

"You're right. I get so intense sometimes, I even bore myself."

"Want to walk out on the pier after work? The sunsets have been beautiful." I wanted desperately to spend some time with her.

"I don't think so."

"Come on. We'll keep it light. Nothing heavy. I promise." She smiled and shook her head yes.

It was a beautiful, but chilly, fall night. The sun was beginning to set, projecting an orange and yellow sky over the slick, dark blue water. As we walked onto the pier, we were silent. When we reached the water's edge, she shivered. We stopped to look at the surfers catching their last waves of the day. "It's beautiful, isn't it?" she said, her teeth chattering from the cold around her. I got behind her, to fend off the wind, and put my arms on the railing, catching her between them. She didn't turn around, and kept her back toward me, but I felt her lean against me. "I could stay like this all night," she whispered. I thought that would be more than okay with me.

We stood there for a long time just feeling our bodies against each other. It was heaven being so close to her. "We'd better get back before I do or say something I'll regret," Kathy whispered. I kissed the back of her head gently and reluctantly let my arms drop to my side.

I walked her to her car. She was quiet all the way back. When she opened her car door, she turned to me. "Why don't you plan on coming over for dinner on Saturday?"

"I'd love to. What time?"

"How bout 6:00. I'll write out the directions for you and leave them on your desk.

Her house was only fifteen minutes away, but it seemed like an eternity. I hit every red light and swore out loud each time I had to stop. I didn't want to be late.

I wondered if Kathy's brother would be there. I had met him briefly at the office. He was a very tall, nice-looking man with bright red hair that he wore down to his shoulders. He had a rust-colored beard with a mustache to match, a very muscular body, and a friendly smile.

When he answered the door, I tried to hide my disappointment. "Come on in," he said warmly. "Kathy's picking up a pizza. She'll be right back." He took my jacket and gave me a tour of the house. It was an upside-down house. Except for the master bedroom, the other bedrooms were downstairs and the living area was upstairs. It was painted in light and dark blues with white trim. The furniture was old, but comfortable. Most of it didn't match.

We had never talked about religion and I was surprised to see the walls covered with religious themes, including a big painting of the Resurrection over the fireplace. John seemed to sense what I was thinking. "Everyone seems surprised when they see these pictures. I know that Kathy doesn't talk about it much but we were brought up in a Christian home with strong Christian values. She's really a very spiritual person and has a strong faith in God. We don't go to church, but we often read together from the Bible." I felt a little embarrassed and a little hurt. I naively thought she shared all of her important feelings with me. As we sat down, I heard a car drive up and minutes later Kathy walked in carrying two pizzas. She gave me a quick hug hello. "Did John show you around?" I assured her that he was a great host. "Well, are you hungry? The pizza's getting cold."

John was an architect and loved his work. He talked non-stop about some of the designs he was working on. I listened but didn't understand a lot of it Besides, I just wanted to be alone with Kathy. After we finished eating she turned to him. "John, would you mind cleaning up? I want to take Susan for a walk up the hill."

"No not at all. Go ahead."

She handed me my jacket and we headed out. No one was in sight and as we began walking, she took my hand. I thought it was a warm and intimate gesture. I didn't say anything, but my heart was racing. I could hardly breathe. "I want to show you something beautiful." At the end of the street was a pathway leading up a very steep incline. She walked ahead of me, kind of pulling me along behind her. I teased her about being in better shape that I was, using it as a pun for getting up the hill, but she knew what I meant. I thought she had a great figure.

When we got to the top, she smiled. "Look!"

I looked over her shoulder and gasped as I saw the lights of the city and the ocean beyond. The moon was so bright I could almost see the reflections of the boats as they were coming into the harbor. "I love it up here. It's my special place." She turned and looked into my eyes. "I wanted to share it with you."

"It truly is beautiful." I touched her face gently. "And so are you."

She turned away for a moment but then looked back quickly. "I've thought about you so much since we had lunch in the car that day. I'm very drawn to you, but I don't know if I could ever accept a gay lifestyle. It goes against everything I've always learned and believed. And I don't want to hurt you." She turned away again, facing the lights, and sat down. I stood there for a moment just looking at her. I decided to take a risk. I sat down behind her with my legs on each side of her body. I pulled her back so that she was leaning against me and I kissed her cheek lightly. I was hoping she didn't feel my body trembling, especially when she put her hands on my legs and started rubbing them lightly." You're really cuddly," she whispered. "It's wonderful."

We sat there like that for a long time. I broke the silence. "I was surprised to see the pictures in your living room. You never talked about religion."

"Are you religious at all?"

"I believe in God if that's what you mean."

"Do you believe he punishes people for their sins."

I knew where she was going. "I don't think loving someone is a sin." "It is if they're the same sex."

"It's men that made that up, not God." For a moment I felt really anxious, but quickly pushed the feeling away. I didn't want anything to ruin these moments with her.

"I'll have to think about that." Then, "We'd better get back. John will think we got kidnapped or something."

We walked back in silence. When we got to her front door, she pulled me to her and kissed me. It took me by surprise and it was awkward. "Let's try that again," I whispered. Her lips were parted slightly, just enough for the tips of our tongues to touch. And when they did, it felt like we melted together, clinging to each other, like we belonged that way forever.

"I really tried not to kiss you, but I honestly felt powerless to resist," she said when our lips finally parted.

"I feel the same way about you," I answered, keeping my lips close to hers. "It really frightens me to be so out of control."

"Don't be afraid. I won't hurt you."

She just smiled and pulled me close again.

"No matter what happens between us in the future, Kathy, I'll never forget this night." I turned and walked toward my car, but looked back at her one more time. She was still watching me. I didn't want to leave her. I wanted to run back and grab her and take her home with me. It was then I knew my life would never be the same.

Lynn was up when I got home. "Where have you been so late?" I avoided her question. "What are you still doing up?"

"I went out with Joe. I just got back a few minutes ago." She paused. "You were out with Kathy, weren't you?"

"I went up to her house for dinner and met her brother. He's a really nice guy." I didn't want to say more. This was such a special, private thing to me.

She looked at me pensively. "You're falling in love with her, aren't you?" "I'm not sure," I answered vaguely, going to my room. She followed me and sat next to me on my bed. "Look. I'm worried about you. I don't want you to get hurt."

"I won't," I snapped back, annoyed that she wouldn't leave me alone.

"She's straight, Susan. Or have you forgotten? Why do you do this to yourself? You know it's not going to go anywhere."

I let down my guard and faced her. "You're right. I never got anywhere with you, did I?"

"That's different. You knew from the beginning that I was just fooling around. And you weren't in love with me."

"And I'm not in love with her. I can handle this. Really." I wanted her to back off. It was none of her business.

"I don't know why you just can't fall for a nice lesbian like other normal lesbians do?" We both laughed. "You really deserve to be loved back -- completely. And it's not going to happen with her."

We'll see, I thought. We'll see.

Chapter Six

I SPENT THE WEEKEND PREOCCUPIED WITH thoughts of Kathy. I had so many questions. How would getting involved affect our working relationship? Would she ever consider living with me? Would she tell her brother about us? I knew that my attraction for her was so strong, that, even with all my reservations about getting involved with a straight woman again, I wouldn't be able to resist. If it's a mistake, I would just have to face the consequences. What's the worst thing that could happen? After all, I've had a broken heart before. Broken hearts heal. Wouldn't it be better to be able to love her for a while than never to have that chance? I felt completely out of control. Was I being a total idiot?

I got to the office early Monday morning. My heart started to beat faster as I pulled into the parking lot and saw her car. When I walked by her office and looked in, she was working on something and didn't see me come in. "Good morning." She looked up, startled, then smiled.

"I didn't expect to see you here so early." She tried to sound cheerful. "I wanted to get an early start on things," I lied.

She walked over to the door and shut it. "We should talk about the other night."

"We don't have to." She looked so serious that I was sure she was going to tell me it was over before it even got started. I think she knew I was nervous.

"I'm not going to tell you that I don't want to see you outside of work, but we really have to keep it separate. Do you think you can do that?"

36

"You mean, you don't want anyone to know about us, right?" I was so relieved!

"Not until I feel more comfortable about it."

"Actually, in case you haven't noticed, I'm real good at keeping secrets. You don't have to worry."

"I know. I probably didn't even have to bring it up."

"You know, I don't even know how you like to spend your time. Maybe we don't have anything in common."

"Oh, I doubt that," she laughed. "Can we have lunch later?" "That would be great. Should I meet you there or go together?

"Together."

It was hard to concentrate on my work and the morning seemed to drag on forever. Apparently, she felt the same way. She showed up at 11:15. We went to a local restaurant and had just finished ordering. "How did you know you were gay?" she asked as the waiter walked away from the table

"It didn't happen all at once. I think it was a slow process. It's funny but I've talked to a lot of gay women about this. I even went to see a gay counselor a couple of times. And when I asked them when they knew they were gay, they all answered, 'I've always known'. It wasn't that way for me. For me, it's been a choice. I think that some people really are genetically gay and some people choose to be in same sexed relationships because of their life circumstances. Maybe the more accurate term is bisexual for people like me. But I don't much care what people call it. And I'm tired of trying to figure it out. I just know that I prefer to be with women."

"So, what were your circumstances?".

"I think it was a combination of things. My older brother has always been 'girl crazy'. I mean, he would screw anyone in a skirt. My family had a recreation room in the basement of our house and there were windows that led out to the backyard. My sister and I would go out there once in a while when we knew he had a girl down there and watched through the window. I was only twelve and Annie was ten. For a long time we couldn't figure out what they were doing. Then we would hear him on the phone with his friends talking about how much sex he got the night before. And they'd laugh together as they shared their sexual escapades.

When I got older and boys started asking me out, I would go, but I'd be furious if they tried to do anything sexual. I went through high school dating a lot of different guys. But if they tried to touch my breast or reach under my skirt, I would drop them like a ton of bricks. It wasn't until years later I realized that I never took it as a compliment when boys found me sexually attractive. I just thought they wanted sex -- with anyone. I just happened to be the girl with them that night. I'm not sure I ever got over that."

She was totally absorbed by what I was saying. When I finished, she said, "This is all so new to me. Do you mind me asking you all these questions?"

"No, not at all. Actually, I think it helps me understand myself better. Some of the things I share with you, I've never really said out loud before. I love that you want to know so much about me. I want to know about you too."

She reached for my hand under the table. "I want to know everything about you. You never talk about your family. Do they live out here?"

"I really don't have much of a family left. My dad died when I was ten. He had a massive heart attack on his way to work one day. My mother and sister were killed in a car crash five years ago. They were on their way to the Grand Canyon." As I went into details about my childhood and the things that happened to my family, tears came to her eyes, but not to mine. I still couldn't cry. Every time I told the story, it always felt as though I was talking about someone else. It just didn't feel real to me. Even after all this time.

When I finished, she said, "Oh Susan. How awful for you. How did you ever process all of that?"

"I'm not sure I have. I just try not to think about it. I went to therapy for a while, but I didn't think it was doing much good so I dropped out.

"How long ago was that?" "Five years."

"Susan, I'm so sorry. It breaks my heart that you had to go through all that." "I have wonderful memories of them. It helps to think that they're together and that someday I'll see them again." "I'm sure that you will."

On the way back, she looked worried. "Is something wrong, Kathy?"

"My parents called last night from Kansas. My father has to come out here on business, so my mom's going to come with him to spend some time with me."

"When are they coming?"

"Tomorrow. Dave gave me the rest of the week off. I really love my parents and like to see them but that means I won't be able to see you for a while."

I was crushed! Could I really survive a whole week without seeing her? I felt lonely already. I also felt sad. I didn't doubt for a minute that if I were a man she'd want me to meet her family. All I said was, "I'll miss you too, Kath."

I didn't get to see her much the rest of the day and we said a quick goodbye before she had to leave. I was very busy at work the week she was gone, which made the time go by faster. I couldn't tell you what I did. My thoughts were consumed with her. I laid in bed at night and relived our first kiss over and over. I'd touch myself in my most sensitive places and imagine that I was touching her. And I realized that for the first time in my life, I was truly in love.

One night Lynn knocked on my bedroom door. "Are you ok in there," she asked opening it. "What's going on, Susan? You've been moping around all week. Have a lovers' quarrel?"

"Hardly. I told you, she's straight."

"Well, maybe this will cheer you up. This telegram just came for you." "Telegram! Who would send me a telegram?"

"Open it and find out."

I laughed. "Remember that scene in Funny Girl when Barbra Streisand gets a telegram and says 'The only time people send telegrams is when it's bad news'." I just looked at the envelope.

"For god sakes, open it," Lynn said impatiently. I opened it, unfolded the paper inside, and read:

When I'm with you the feeling of being special is overpowering. You make me feel joy and happiness like I've never felt before.

My heart races, my eyes fill with tears. I want so to share with you my love. It was signed: Kathy

I read it over several times. "Well?" Lynn asked.

"It's from Kathy," I said joyfully. "She loves me."

I couldn't wait to get back to work and see her. "So, how did it go with your parents?"

"My dad was busy with business, so I spent most of the time with my mom. We did a lot of shopping and went to a few movies. My mom is real quiet, so I always have to carry most of the conversation." She paused. "To tell you the truth, it was torture. All I wanted to do was talk about you. But I couldn't."

I turned and shut the door. She came out from behind her desk and just stood there looking at me. "You're making me nervous," I said, wanting to reach out and hold her.

"I just forgot how really beautiful you are," she said, touching my face. "You're really lovely."

Then she backed off. "We can't do this here." "I know." But I didn't want her to stop.

As I turned to leave, I looked back at her. She had already returned to her desk, but her eyes were still on me. "I loved the telegram."

She smiled. "See you later."

The women's group was going well and we both enjoyed being part of the interaction and close bonds that the women were forming with each other.

Each week, Kathy gave me more responsibility, and within a few months, we truly were co-therapists. Sometimes, we gave them exercises to do together to build trust. One night we planned a trust walk. As the women assembled, we paired them off in twos. Then we blindfolded one of them and instructed the other one to lead her partner around the building, making sure she didn't bump into anything or get hurt. "Obviously, the purpose of the walk is to experience how much you trust your partner to keep you safe in a vulnerable situation." There were three pairs. We instructed the "leaders" to meet back in the group room in ten minutes, "and then we'll switch. The leader will become the blindfolded partner."

After they left, Kathy approached me with a blindfold. "Let's do it." I hesitated. "Come on. I'll go first." I carefully wrapped the blindfold around her eyes and led her out of the room. She giggled as she slowly followed, holding tightly to my hand. "This is harder than I thought it would be." The building was quite large with wide hallways. I didn't want to run into the other women, so I led her to the stairway.

"Careful, now, we're going downstairs." Her other hand was trying to feel something solid, but I stopped her. "No cheating. Put your hand down." I physically and verbally guided her slowly down the steps. She was smiling, but this was obviously difficult for her. When we got to the bottom, I led her into one of the offices, making sure that no one else was around. "Okay, this is the hardest part," I said, and, without warning, kissed her softly on her mouth. She pulled away immediately, obviously not expecting it.

"No fair," she whispered, taking off the blindfold.

"You're not mad, are you Kath? I couldn't resist. No one else is around. I made sure of it."

She smiled. "No. I'm not mad. It just caught me off guard. We'd better get up there."

The women had returned and were chattering away about their experiences. "Okay," I said. "Now let's switch." They blindfolded their partners and excitedly walked out of the room. Kathy crocked her finger in the "come here" stance. "You don't hold a grudge, do you?" I said jokingly.

"You'll find out."

I was nervous as she began to lead me out the door, but I knew I was safe and easily followed her. This surprised her. "You're really pretty relaxed for someone who's in big trouble!"

"I'm not worried," I replied calmly. "I'd go anywhere with you."

CHAPTER SEVEN

I WAS BEGINNING TO FEEL MORE competent at my job and more confident in my relationship with Kathy. She was a wonderful supervisor and teacher. As I completed the home studies of the foster parents, she supported me every step of the way. She never seemed to tire of answering my questions, and more importantly, she gave me the positive feedback I needed. She taught me how to do effective interviews and put people at ease. I felt more comfortable with my clients and I think they sensed it. As they built up their trust in me, they opened their hearts. It was a beautiful thing to be part of.

I worked late every night on the training class for the new foster parents, which was due to start in a few weeks. We were teaching them the parenting skills they would need once they started getting children in their homes and how to deal with some of the special problems a foster child might have tried to fit into their family. I was very excited about it. Once the foster parents were trained and certified, we could begin placing children. This was the part of the job I was really looking forward to. It was interesting interviewing and getting to know the foster parents, but it was the children that both Kathy and I wanted to work with. I was thrilled when she agreed to help me with the class. It was another block of time we'd get to spend together. She assured me that I would be the main teacher; she'd just be there for support. She knew I was worried about carrying it by myself. It was her way of showing me how much she cared.

When I walked into the room the first night of the training, I had a sense of accomplishment that I never felt before. "As I stand here and look out at all of you, I feel a sense of pride for recruiting such a wonderful group of people for this program." When they smiled and applauded, my initial nervousness went away. The classes went exceedingly well. The parents participated fully in all of the exercises and were relaxed with each other. It made the time fun as well as interesting. When Kathy and I walked out of the building together after the classes, she would smile and tell me what a terrific job I was doing. We'd say goodnight with a squeeze of our hands or a quick hug. I'd usually wait until she drove off before I headed home. Most of the time I wanted to follow her, but I decided in the beginning, that if the relationship went any further, she would have to make the next move. I didn't want to push her into something she wasn't sure of. But I was starting to feel so impatient. Sometimes it was hard to hold back.

We had a party for the foster parents on the last night of the class. They were excited that the program was finally getting started and that they would have children in their homes very shortly. They had grown quite close and even exchanged phone numbers. Kathy and I stayed to clean up after the party and talked non-stop about how well everything was going. When the last dish was put away, I felt a little sad that it was ending. She seemed to sense this and put her arm around me. I wanted to be closer to her so I put my head on her shoulder. She pulled away quickly. I wanted to stop her, but she had already started walking towards the door. "Let's get out of here."

We walked out of the building together as we usually did and I stopped by her car for our usual hug. This time she said, "Can you sit here for a while with me? I don't feel like going home yet."

"Sure." I would have sat with her all night if she wanted me to.

She opened the door and I got in. I watched her slowly walk to the driver's side and slide in next to me. She looked at me in that serious way that I was beginning to get used to. "Are you struggling with this relationship as much as I am?"

"I don't know. How hard are you struggling?" I felt nervous. Finally she was going to talk about it. I knew something significant was about to happen. She laughed. "You have this uncanny ability to make me tell you more than I had planned." I didn't answer. "On the one hand, I'd like to spend more time with you outside of work and just see where it takes us. But I think I know where it will take us and I don't want to end up hurting you."

"Are you sure you'd end up hurting me?" Maybe she'd end up loving me!

"I just don't think I could ever live a gay lifestyle on a permanent basis. It would interfere with everything I've always wanted -- a home, children, a husband. I don't know how to fit you into that." She paused. "Aren't you going to say anything?"

"I think the big difference between me and you is that I don't think much about the future. It's too complicated for me to make decisions that way. I just usually go by what I'm feeling now."

"And what are you feeling now?"

I turned and looked right at her. "Don't you know? I love you." We just sat there, looking at each other for a long time. It felt like we were making love with just our eyes.

"Come here," she said softly, holding out her arms. I moved closer to her and let her pull me the rest of the way. She hugged me for a long time and then she whispered, "Let's get in the backseat." Even though she had reservations, I knew she had made a decision. I didn't have any reservations, but I was still scared to death. I was starting to feel again. And, this time, I had no intention of running away.

I pulled away from her and reached for the door. She did the same on the other side. She had a Volkswagen Bug so there wasn't much more room in the back than there was in the front. I suggested we go back in the building. "No, I'd feel uncomfortable in there." I stood outside the car as she was ducking her head to get in the backseat. Then I followed her in. There was little room for our feet, so I tried to pull her legs over to my side and maneuver my head over to her side. We ended up very cramped so we started shuffling our bodies again. This time I ended up with my back against the front seat, but I was able to pull myself closer to her and she ended up almost underneath me. We both took another minute to shift our legs to a more comfortable position and when she was still, I kissed her. When my lips first touched hers, she opened her mouth so that we molded perfectly together.

We seemed to be in perfect sync, going in tandem from our lips barely touching to deep, passionate kisses with an urgency I had never experienced before. We held each other, barely moving, except for our mouths. If I felt her pulling away, I followed her, not letting her mouth escape mine, until she would cling to me again and again. When we finally pulled apart she said in a whisper, "I'm not fragile. I won't break if you touch me." Her skin was as smooth as it was soft. I unbuttoned the first two buttons of her blouse and softly touched her bare neck and the top of her chest. She pulled her body away so that I could unbutton the rest of her blouse. I opened it and put my hand on her breast. I could feel her nipple harden under her bra and she moaned as I began to lightly rub it with my thumb. I reached my other hand behind her back and unhooked her bra. When it was free I pulled it up over her breasts. They were full, but firm and I went from one to the other caressing them with my fingers.

She kept whispering in my ear, "Yes...don't stop...that feels wonderful." Suddenly, her body began to quiver under me and she struggled to push her groin against me. "Oh, my God, my God!"

I wasn't sure what she wanted, so I just kept stroking her breasts, harder now as she pulled me to her mouth and kissed me with a passion I could never have imagined. Her body was thrusting against me now in a way that I thought was beautiful. I pushed against her so that she could apply more pressure. She was moving faster now, and suddenly her body lost control and went into convulsions as she reached a climax. I held her close, and when she finally relaxed, she took a deep breath and turned her head away. I put my hand on her cheek. She turned back and looked at me. I spoke first.

"That was incredible."

"I knew my breasts were sensitive, but I've never been touched like that before. It was so tender and sweet. I felt so loved. The feeling just kind of swept me away."

I hugged her close again and we stayed that way for several minutes. When I looked up from her for the first time, I laughed, as all of the windows in the car were completely fogged up. "I guess we didn't have to worry about anybody seeing us together." She smiled and then struggled to get up. She hooked up her bra and started buttoning her blouse. I just watched.

"So, does this mean you've made a decision?" I asked her directly so that I could be sure.

"What do you think?"

"No fair, answering a question with a question." "Can we just take this day by day for now?" "That's all we can do. Of course, it's okay."

She was serious again. "Are you okay? I feel kind of selfish."

"Yeah. I told you. It was wonderful. I've never had anyone respond to me that way before. Besides, I'm so cramped in this car that the lower part of my body is completely numb."

She laughed. "I guess we should try to get out."

When I tried to stand up, my knees buckled. She caught me, and we hugged again. "I don't want to leave you," I said as we let go of each other.

"I know. It's hard for me too."

As she got back into the driver's seat and sat down, I closed the door behind her. "Try not to think too much," I said very seriously. I knew she might have reservations and regrets about what just happened.

"You're getting to know me pretty well, huh." She started her car. "I'll call you tomorrow morning. Maybe we can meet for dinner or something."

"That would be great." All the way home, I wondered what she meant by "or something."

The phone rang at 9:30. I was taking advantage of a Saturday and sleeping late. Lynn knocked on my door. "It's for you. It's Kathy."

"It's a beautiful day for a hike," she said excitedly. "Can you be ready in an hour? I'll pick you up."

"Sure," I said smiling. "Are we making a day of it?" "Why not? See you soon."

I raced into the shower and quickly dressed. I never figured her for a hiker, but then, I never figured her for a lot of things.

I was waiting outside when she drove up. She was wearing a wide rimmed brown hat, jeans, a sweater, and hiking boots.

"You look adorable," I said, hopping into her Bug. "No one has ever called me adorable before."

"Do you mind?" She smiled and shook her head.

"I made a decision on the way home yesterday." I held my breath and waited. "I'm not going to be heavy and intense about us. I'm just going to have fun and enjoy being with you." Thank God, I thought. At that point, I didn't think I could live without her.

We had a wonderful time, just walking and getting to know each other better. We shared funny stories about our families and laughed together until it hurt. She had a terrific sense of humor, and enjoyed teasing me in a caring way that I grew to love.

She talked about her younger sister, whom she described as "beautiful." "She was the beautiful one and I was the smart one." She lived in Kansas, near her parents, and was planning to visit Kathy in a few months.

"I can't wait to meet her."

"Well, I'll introduce you to her, if I can meet your brother."

"No way. I wouldn't let him near you with a 10-foot pole. Don't even joke about that!"

"Look who's getting intense!" she laughed

We spent the next few weeks seeing each other as much as we could. At work, we continued to share several projects, which made it easy to have lunch together. After work, we'd go out to dinner or to a movie. One night we even went roller skating. To my surprise, she was pretty athletic and enjoyed playing tennis and golf. On her birthday, I got her a new tennis racquet, which pleased her immensely.

We held hands in the movies and hugged each other before going home, but she didn't suggest anything sexual and I didn't push it. Besides everything else, we were becoming good friends. This became a precious part of our relationship. Just being with her was more than enough for the moment. I didn't think about tomorrow.

CHAPTER EIGHT

WE WERE SITTING ACROSS FROM each other at a restaurant on the beach, taking advantage of the beautiful, spring evening. There were surfers on the water enjoying the unusually warm weather. They were in bathing suits rather than wet suits, so you could see their muscular bodies as they stood on their boards with their arms outstretched. Kathy smiled as she watched them, then looked back at me. "I can still look," she joked. I smiled back at her feeling that we shared a wonderful secret together. We were quiet for a long time.

She broke the silence. "John's going on a fishing trip Monday. He'll be away for a week. How would you like to stay with me while he's gone?"

"Really!" I didn't even have to think about it. "I'd love to." I wanted to ask if this meant that she decided to get more involved with me, but I figured I'd find out soon enough. I couldn't wait for the week to start. The thought of being with her every night for a whole week was thrilling. I was ecstatic!

Lynn came into my room as I packed. "I think you're making a big mistake."

"I know you do," I replied, not looking up.

She sat down on my bed. "Have you really thought this through, Susan?"

"I haven't thought about anything else for the last month." I stopped and sat down next to her. "I don't think feelings like this happen very often." I spoke slowly and carefully. "And I know it can turn out badly. But if I pass up the chance to have a relationship with someone I

50

absolutely adore, I'm not sure I'll ever have the chance again. And even if it doesn't work out, I think it will be better than wondering forever what could have been."

She put her arm around me. "Well, if you need me, I'll be here for you. I truly hope it does work out for you. I don't want to lose you as a roommate, but I want you to be happy."

"Thanks, Lynn. That means a lot to me."

I was late and out of breath when I rang the bell. She gave me a warm hug when she opened the door. We stood in the hallway for a moment, just looking at each other. "I'm really nervous," I finally said.

"So am I. Come on in." She took my hand. "I made dinner." I put my suitcase down and followed her up the stairs. She had candles on the table along with flowers and a bottle of wine. She opened the wine and poured two glasses. She handed one to me and said, "Here's to a great week." We clicked glasses and each took a sip. "I planned some things that we can do together-- we can work on this 1000 piece jigsaw puzzle, we can play cards and Scrabble. I love to play Scrabble."

"Did I ever tell you that I came in 7th in the Ohio State Scrabble tournament last year?"

"Well, maybe we'll skip Scrabble." We both laughed.

"Come on to the table. I'll bet you're hungry." She made spaghetti with meatballs and salad.

"I haven't had a home-cooked meal like this in a long time. It's delicious. Thank you."

"I really love to cook, but with work and all, I don't get a chance to do it very often."

"Is that why you snuck out early today? I thought you had an appointment." "I lied."

"So you're not the goodie-goodie you pretend to be, huh?" She laughed. "Is that what I was pretending to be?"

After dinner I helped her with the dishes, then we moved to the couch in her living room. I felt a lot calmer than when I first came in, but I could tell that she was still nervous. "So, where do you want me to sleep?" I asked, thinking it would ease the tension to get things out in the open.

"With me." Her directness always surprised me. I'd never met anyone like her in that respect.

"I'm just making sure," I said quietly. "Want to watch some TV?" She asked.

I wanted to say 'No I just want to go to bed,' but instead I said, "What's on?" "I don't know, let's look." She got out a TV guide and started looking through the pages. After a minute she looked up at me. "Wanna go to bed?" I

shook my head yes.

"My suitcase is downstairs."

"You can use the bathroom down there if you want to. You'd have more room for your things."

I unpacked my sundries, brushed my teeth and headed back upstairs with the rest of my stuff. She was sitting up in her bed, with the bedspread at her waist, leaning against several pillows. She had on a white nightgown with thin shoulder straps that fit her frame tightly. The silky material came just over her breasts in the front so that her arms and chest were bare. I stared at her for several seconds before I spoke. "I've imagined you like this hundreds of times, but you're even more lovely." I couldn't wait to hold her.

I took off my tennis shoes and socks, and slipped off my sweater and jeans. I was wearing a large tee shirt underneath my sweater that came down to my thighs, with no bra. I pulled back the bedspread on the other side of the bed and got in. She had been watching me undress, but didn't say a word. I sat next to her with my hands in my lap and smiled widely, "Now what should we do?" She didn't laugh.

I reached for the lamp on my side of the bed and quickly turned it off. There was a night light coming from the bathroom that made the room light enough so that we could still see each other clearly.

"Well, goodnight," she said as she laid down and turned her back to me. I could tell that she was teasing. Her nightgown came down to her waist in the back, leaving it totally exposed. I wrapped my body around her, and put one arm around her shoulders and the other around her waist. I purposely didn't touch her breasts. Neither of us moved for a long time.

Finally, I started kissing her shoulder, then her back. My tongue ran over every inch, with long, soft kisses in between. She squirmed, but I didn't stop. I kissed her again and again as the realization that I was finally with her began to sink in. When my mouth reached the back of her neck, she moaned. Then she turned around to face me. Our lips met and our arms wrapped around each other. I could feel her breasts against me. Our bodies adjusted so that everything connected. I reached up to slide the straps of her nightgown down her arms and pulled the top of it beneath her breasts so that they were exposed. I kept kissing her but pulled my body away so that I could put both of my hands between us to cup both of her breasts at once. Her nipples were already hard and I rubbed them with the tips of my fingers very softly. She reached up under my tee shirt and lightly touched one of my breasts. It was like an electric shock going through me. Then she reached for the other one and stroked and caressed them both. I still had both of my hands on her and we moved our bodies in tandem, loving the wonder of each other's touch.

She pulled away from my mouth and smiled. "I've never done anything like this. What's it called?"

"I think it's called mutual masturbation." We both laughed. It broke the tension.

"Do you know how long I've dreamed of being with you like this?" she said in a whisper. I don't think she expected an answer.

"No longer than I have. I don't think I've ever been with anyone that I've loved who loved me back in the same way. What an incredible feeling!"

"So you think I love you, huh?" she teased. "I've never felt anything stronger."

She kissed me then, and I responded by pulling her close. She put her hands on the bottom of my tee shirt. "Let's take this off." I sat up to let her pull it over my head. Her nightgown was still pulled down below her breasts, and I reached my hands over to pull it down the rest of the way. She lifted her body up so that I could take it down over her hips. I looked at her beneath me. I could hardly breathe. Her body was beautiful, with smooth white skin and full breasts. I loved the way it curved perfectly down to her hips. "You're embarrassing me," she said softly and pulled me down on top of her. Our lips met again, perfectly, as we intuitively adjusted to each other's kiss.

Slowly, we explored each other's bodies with our hands, like one explores a precious and delicate treasure. I touched her the way I loved to be touched and she did the same to me. When I put my hand between her legs, I pulled my mouth from hers and kissed her neck and the front of her shoulders. I worked my way down to her breast and as I took it into my mouth, she pressed her groin against my hand. As I gently rubbed my tongue over her nipple, she guided my fingers to her most sensitive spot. I started rubbing it in little circular motions as I continued to love her breast with my mouth. I stroked it softly at first, then harder, as she pushed against me. In a moment, she started jerking and shaking as she began her climax. I tried to keep stroking her, but her body was shaking so much that I couldn't keep contact. So, I just put my arms around her and hugged her close. I was so excited by her climax, that I was very close to an orgasm myself. So I got into a position where I could rub my groin against her leg and climaxed easily.

When we were both quiet, I said, "Let's just stay like this all night." "Yes," she whispered. We fell asleep in each other's arms.

CHAPTER NINE

"WHY DON'T WE TELL THEM that my apartment caught fire and you offered me a place to stay while they were making the repairs."

"Oh right, they'll really believe that!"

We were driving to work together trying to figure out what we were going to tell our co-workers if they saw us. I could tell that Kathy was more worried about it than I was. I cared more about her than about what anyone thought.

"How 'bout this? There was a rape in your neighborhood and John felt uneasy about leaving you alone. So he wanted to have someone stay with you."

"That has possibilities. Maybe we should just say we're in love and I invited you to stay at my place while my brother was gone so that we could be together every night."

She said it with such a straight face that for a second I thought she was serious. "Okay. I'll say that," I replied, matching her serious tone.

"You would not! You've always said that you don't want people to know." "That was before I met you. I'd love to tell people now. I think they'd be jealous of me that I have such a wonderful person in my life." "Maybe someday, sweetheart, but I can't do it now."

"I know. Listen, why do we have to say anything? If we start trying to explain ourselves, it will probably look more suspicious."

"But what if they ask?"

"Just laugh and say, 'Yeah, I'm a big chicken. John went fishing so I asked Susan to stay with me'. Then just walk away and don't look guilty."

"Yeah, I've been practicing my don't look guilty look for weeks now. What do you think?" She had a slight smile on her face.

"Get rid of the smile."

"Like this?" She kept a straight face and raised one of her eyebrows. "That's perfect."

"So," she said, satisfied that we had solved our first problem together. "What should we do tonight?"

"You're kidding, aren't you?" We had just pulled into the parking lot and Steve was right behind us. "Okay," I said. "Here's your chance."

"Hi girls," he said cheerfully.

"Hi Steve. How are you?" I answered casually, trying to set a good example.

"Is your car in the shop, Kathy?"

"No, John went fishing and I hate to be alone so Susan is staying with me for the week. We're getting a lot of work done." He kind of smirked as he held the door open for us.

"You blew it," I whispered.

She frowned. "I overdid it with the work stuff, huh."

"Don't worry about it. Who cares what they think anyway." I gave her hand a quick squeeze. "See you later."

The message said, "Call ASAP". I dialed the number.

Her name was Patsy Parker. She said she had a thirteen-year-old daughter that she wanted evaluated for the program. I made an appointment to see her later that day.

The address was in a dilapidated section of Long Beach. The houses were very old and run down. The lawns were more like weeds, wild and uneven. The outside yard of the Parker house was filled with old junk -- a broken bicycle, a rusty lawn mower, broken toys, and torn furniture. Patsy came to the door as I walked up. She was a tiny woman, about 35, with thin, stringy brown hair, a long nose, thin lips and cold green eyes. She didn't smile as she said hello and let me in. The living room was dark and dusty. Piles of dirty laundry and old toys covered the floor. The furniture was very old and worn. Nothing in the room remotely matched.

She motioned me to sit down. Then she sat in a chair opposite me.

"What do I have to do to put my daughter in a foster home?" she asked immediately.

"Well, I need to get some background information to see if she would be appropriate for our program. Why do you want to put her in foster care?"

"Actually," she said coldly, "I'd like to get rid of her all together, but my husband says she's too old to adopt." What a bitch!, I thought. I couldn't imagine what this little girl could have done to make her mother want to get rid of her! I was horrified at the thought!

"But why?"

"My husband and I have five other children. I got pregnant with Teresa before I met him. He married me before she was born but he's always resented her and, well, she's so different from our other children. She just doesn't fit into this family. We don't love her in the same way that we love our other kids." I had a lump in my throat as I remembered how I felt about my own mother's betrayal. But at least she never wanted to give me away!

"Does Teresa know that you feel this way?"

"I don't think so. She thinks Ed is her father. We never told her anything different. Now that she's getting older, she wants things. You know, like dressy clothes and things for her room. We can't afford to get her all that stuff. So she sits around and sulks all the time. It gets on our nerves."

"Have you thought about family counseling? Surely this can be worked out."

"I told you. Ed doesn't want to spend his money on Teresa. Our other children are going to need things." Again, I was taken back by her coldness towards her child.

"Why did you wait so long to make this decision?" "Ed thought he'd grow to love her. But he never did."

"But you love her, don't you?" I was livid that she wasn't defending her daughter!

"I guess I do. But she's a hard kid. She's so moody. I don't like her around me much."

"But most teenagers are moody. Mrs. Parker, are you sure you've thought this through? Giving her away would be devastating for your child.

"Look. It sounds like you're trying to talk me out of this. If you won't take her, I'll call someone else. We've made up our minds." She sounded so final that it made me back off. But my heart broke for this little girl.

"Have you told Teresa?"

"No. We thought you'd do that." It was hard to believe that this lady was for real. She was heartless!

"Well, I could be there, but you'll have to explain it to her." "We don't want to tell her about Ed not being her father."

"You don't have to do that right away, but eventually she should know. Is Ed on her birth certificate?"

"Yes. At the time we thought that was best."

"Well, then legally, that will make the process easier." At least something will be easier, I thought. "We'll need to set up a time for me to meet with both Teresa and Ed. Then we can go from there." I took some background information on Teresa and left some forms for them to go over. I also left some literature about our program and said a quick goodbye. Although Patsy was nothing like my mother, they did have one thing in common. They both sacrificed a child for a man's love.

I felt sad all the way back to the office.

"I think I have a child to place," I announced walking into Kathy's office. I didn't tell her how I was really feeling. I didn't want to come across as negative and I didn't want her to think that my own background would interfere in my work.

"Great. You can tell me about it on the way home. Let's get out of here."

As we were walking out, she smiled. "I almost forgot. You got a raise today. Something about the agency raising salaries to be competitive with other agencies in the county."

"How much?"

"Thirty dollars a week."

"My God, I'm rich. Before the week is out, I'm taking you out for a great dinner. Now, let me tell you about Teresa."

As I told her about my meeting with Patsy, Kathy tried hard to support me. She minimized my negative feelings about Patsy and Ed and helped me understand how important my role in Teresa's transition to a new family will be.

"Isn't it wonderful that our agency can help kids like Teresa? She doesn't know it now, but this is probably a wonderful chance for her to grow up in a loving environment and reach her full potential. You have to look past today. You have to believe you're doing a good thing for her. If you believe it, when she grows to trust you, she'll believe it too." She was always so positive when it came to the kids. I thought she was a little naive, but I loved her for trying to cheer me up. I hoped her attitude would be catching. I had my doubts that I could handle this without falling apart.

"Kathy, how do I tell a thirteen-year-old child that her parents want to get rid of her?"

"You don't. You just have to be there for her as everything starts to sink in and let her talk -- about anything she wants to. The important thing to get across to her is that you're going to help her through this and that she can trust you."

"But how do I do that?"

"Just be yourself. You have a wonderful ability to get people to open up and trust you. I should know. It may take some time but she'll get the message. Just trust your feelings. You'll do the right thing. I have complete confidence in you."

"You always seem to know exactly what I need. I don't know how I ever got along without you." How I wished I had someone like her around when my family was in such a crisis. I really didn't have anyone to help me through all that pain.

"Me either," she smiled widely. "So how are you going to thank me?" "Oh, I guess I'll think of something," I said with a wink.

"Drive faster. I can't wait to get home."

Doug and Mary Collins were my first choice to take Teresa. I thought they were going to make great foster parents and looked forward to working with them. I knew they wouldn't hesitate at a chance to take any child.

During the training sessions they were very involved and genuinely had a good time doing all the exercises. One night, we role-played how a child might feel when interacting with an angry adult. We had Mary sit on the floor and had Doug stand above her with an angry look on his face, shaking his finger at her. Mary was astonished at how scary it was looking up at him and vowed she would never do that to a child.

They were also very supportive towards the other foster parents in the class. One couple had difficulty with the exercises and had their doubts about completing the training. They told me weeks later that Mary and Doug took them out for coffee after class and helped them understand that we were all in this together and convinced them to stay.

And they were both very supportive towards me. They laughed at all my jokes, and listened intently when I explained the different techniques they could use when dealing with difficult children. At the end of each class, they always thanked me for a very interesting and fun evening. They were thrilled when I told them I was going to place a child in their home and couldn't wait to meet Teresa. They didn't have to wait very long.

Teresa was sitting on the front porch when I drove up. She was small in stature, like her mother, but that was their only similarity. Her hair was light brown and wavy and fell just below her shoulders. Her nose was small and straight. She was wearing blue jeans with holes at the knees and old tennis shoes. And she had the saddest big brown eyes I had ever seen.

"You must be Teresa," I said cheerfully as I approached her. She didn't look up, but she shook her head yes. "I'm Susan." I held my hand out, but she didn't respond. "Did your mom tell you about me?"

"Are you the lady that's going to take me away from my family?" she said in a whisper.

"Is that what your mom told you?" Oh, great! Set me up to be the bad guy! "She said that I couldn't live here anymore because I wanted too many things.

I promised her I wouldn't ask for anything else if I could stay, but she said I should see if I like living with another family better."

"What do you think of that idea?"

"I want to stay here," she said holding back tears. I wanted to comfort her, but it was too soon. I felt if I did, I would scare her away.

"Well, I'm here to talk to your mom and dad about what's best for you. But no matter what they decide, I promise to help you in every way I can." She looked at me for the first time but she didn't say anything. "Why don't you wait here while I talk to them?" But I didn't really want to talk to them. I wanted to get in my car and drive away. It was obvious that this kid was heartbroken. I didn't want to be part of this betrayal.

I walked up the steps and knocked on the door. Ed answered. He was huge --very tall and muscular. His black hair and beard made him look very rugged, like a mountain man. His appearance was in such stark contrast to his wife that it took me off guard. "Hi. I'm Susan Kramer from the Foster Care Agency."

"I know who you are," he said gruffly.

I went inside hesitantly. Patsy was sitting in the living room. "I just met Teresa. She's a lovely child."

"You won't say that when you get to know her better," Ed said, obviously annoyed.

"What makes you say that?" I disliked him as much as I disliked Patsy. "Because she's a brat. She's selfish and spoiled. And she's a little pest." "Now Ed," Patsy said. "She's not that bad."

"If that's how you feel about her, I assume you're in agreement with your wife's decision to place her in a foster home."

"You can't get her out of here fast enough." "Mr. Parker, why do you dislike her so?"

"She's a troublemaker, that's why. And she's got a smart mouth. And the other kids don't get along with her," he said in a very irritated tone of voice.

I thought he was lying. There had to be more to it than that. But I didn't know how to challenge him. So I just said, "I know that you're upset, but I'm just trying to understand what happened in this family to get you both to this point."

"You bet I'm upset. I don't like people nosing around in my business."

"Ed, I told you she was going to ask a lot of questions. Now calm down," his wife urged.

"Mr. and Mrs. Parker, in order for us to place Teresa in a foster home, you're both going to have to agree to participate in counseling. The purpose of our program is to keep families together, not pull them apart. We realize that sometimes parents just need a break. And we're here to help with that."

"Counseling, huh," he snapped. "And what if we don't want her back?" "Hopefully that won't happen, but if it did, then we'd try to find a permanent home for her."

"I explained this to you Ed," Patsy said impatiently. "Remember? You agreed."

He shook his head.

I took out the forms they'd have to fill out and sign for legal purposes. "I'm going to leave these forms here for you to complete. Why don't you look them over now so I can answer any questions that you may have. I'll be back tomorrow to pick them up. Have Teresa's things packed. I'll be picking her up tomorrow too."

"Can't you take her now?" Patsy asked. I was shocked!

"Don't you want to give her a chance to say goodbye to her brothers and sisters?"

"They've already said their goodbyes. And so have we. So you may as well take her. All of her things are packed."

I hesitated for a moment, but agreed to take her. At this point, I couldn't wait to get her away from these horrible people! "You both have to sign the forms. You can mail in the other information. I'll be outside with Teresa." As I walked outside, she was rushing back to the porch. "I guess you heard all of that, huh."

Her cheeks were stained with tears. I sat down next to her and put my arm around her shoulder. "I know it's hard, Kiddo. And I know you don't understand everything. But you're going to love your foster parents and they're going to love you. Their names are Mary and Doug. They're both very kind. You're going to be their first foster child, so they're a little nervous about meeting you. But they're so excited too. They have a lot of love to give to a child like you."

The door opened. "Here are all of the forms," Patsy said holding them out to me. "Now you be good Teresa and mind what people tell you."

"I will, mama." Patsy gave her daughter a quick hug. Teresa tried to cling to her but Patsy pulled away.

"I'll call you in a few days to set up the counseling sessions and visitation schedule. Come on kiddo." I held out my hand. She hung on tightly as we walked to my car. She needed someone to cling to. As we drove off she turned to wave goodbye to her mother, but Patsy had already disappeared into the house. She cried all the way to the Collins' home. I felt awful for her.

Doug and Mary were waiting outside as we drove up. Teresa looked terrified. "We're here, sweetie."

Mary came over to the car and opened the passenger door. "Hi Teresa. I'm Mary." She looked nervous. Who wouldn't be? Heck, I was a wreck this whole day. "And this is Doug, my husband. We're so glad you decided to come and live with us for a while. We've been waiting to share our home with a child like you for a long time. We can't wait to show you your new room."

She looked at me with those big, sad eyes.

"It's Okay. Go on. I'll be right behind you." She walked right over to Doug, who took her hand and led her inside. I filled Mary in on the little information I had on Teresa so far.

"Poor kid. What kind of parents would give up a thirteen-year-old child?"

Well, I know both of you will be great for her. You know, we're going to get to know each other pretty well because I'm going to be here a lot. I hope that's okay with you."

"Of course, Susan. You're always welcome. Even if Teresa wasn't here, you'd be welcome."

"Thanks, Mary. I'll come in and say goodbye."

Teresa came running out of the bedroom. She was smiling. "Come see my room, Susan."

"Oh, it's beautiful." It was pink with a canopy bed and a dressing table with a big mirror on the back. "It's perfect for you! Do you think you'll be okay here, Teresa?"

"I don't know."

She seemed much younger than her thirteen years, both physically and emotionally.

I stooped down, "I know you're going to miss your parents and your brothers and sisters. It's Okay to talk about it with me or Mary or Doug. We understand how hard this is for you and want to help you as much as we can."

She seemed so vulnerable. I wanted to protect her. "They seem real nice."

"They are. And I'm sure they're going to be crazy about you."

She smiled. "Thank you. You're really nice too." She hugged me tightly. "I'm your friend, Teresa. You can talk to me about anything. I'll be back to see you in three or four days. If you want to talk to me before then, just ask Mary for my number."

I was actually pleased with the way things had turned out and felt hopeful that Teresa would be better off with Doug and Mary. And, I felt proud of myself for doing a good job.

"How did it go?" Kathy asked when I got back to the office.

"I'll tell you about it on the way home. But after that, let's not talk about work. I have a special evening planned for you."

CHAPTER TEN

I HAD MIXED FEELINGS DRIVING TO the restaurant. I was looking forward to a wonderful evening with Kathy, but I knew our time together was ending since John would be home the next day. She sensed my sadness and stroked my arm softly. "You're awfully quiet tonight." I didn't answer. "Let's not be sad, Susan. This isn't goodbye."

"I know," I answered, holding back tears. "I'm trying so hard not to let tomorrow ruin the time we have tonight. This has been the most wonderful week of my life."

She squeezed my hand and tried to smile. "Me too." She looked at me for a long time. "You're so beautiful. When you look at me like this, I feel you can read my mind. It's very scary to feel so vulnerable. But very exciting too."

I laughed. "Don't get me started. We'll never get out of the car and I don't know if my legs can take it."

"Ok. Let's go in."

The restaurant was elegantly decorated with beautiful paintings of the California shoreline. The hostess was friendly as she led us to a table that looked out on the water. It reminded me of that first night together on the hill. "I hope you have enough money," she joked. "I don't want to end up washing dishes."

"Don't worry. I just got a raise."

"That raise won't even pay for toilet paper in a place like this."

"It doesn't matter. It was my first professional raise and we're celebrating. Although now that you mention it, it was a little meager."

"Don't complain. It was bigger than mine."

I got serious again. "I'm going to miss this more than anything. I just love talking and joking with you."

"But this won't end, silly."

"I'm selfish. I want it everyday and every night!"

She changed the subject. "I wonder if John caught any fish." I knew she was uncomfortable talking about a long future with me.

But I changed the subject back to us. "Are you going to tell him about us?" "No," she answered without thinking.

I felt hurt and, instead of hiding it like I normally would, I let it show on my face. She tried to fix it. "Not right now anyway. I don't think he'll ever understand, Susan. And I'm not ready to handle that yet. I just want more time with you before I face these heavy issues. Time with you is very precious to me and I want to protect it. This relationship will never survive unless we have a strong foundation."

She was right, of course. "Kathy, I wasn't thinking. I'm really embarrassed that I'm being so selfish and impatient. Sometimes I just forget how hard this must be for you."

She smiled. "You're pretty cute when you're embarrassed."

"Are you flirting with me again?" She obviously didn't want to get into anything heavy.

"It's my favorite thing to do," she said with a wink. "Are you sure?" She knew what I meant.

"Well, maybe my second favorite thing. What's your favorite?"

"Hmmm, let me think." I couldn't help laughing. "It's such a hard choice." "Maybe you haven't done it yet," she said, still smiling.

Where was this going, I thought. "Do you know something I don't know?" "Yes, and I'm not telling."

"Oh, come on. You know you can't keep a secret from me."

We were both having a wonderful time bantering with each other. "This time is different. You won't get me to tell, so forget it."

We ordered a bottle of wine with dinner and after our glasses were filled, she held up hers for a toast. "Here's to you. You make me feel significant in a world of insignificance."

I clicked her glass. "You amaze me sometimes. You're such a treasure." And then, "How do I make you feel significant?"

"You listen to every word I say as if it were the most important thing you've ever heard. I've never experienced that before."

"It's all part of my plan to make me indispensable to you," I teased. "Is it working?"

"If I say yes, are you going to stop?" "I'll never stop," I said emphatically. "Then, yes. What else is in your plan?" "I'm just going to keep you guessing."

She looked over my shoulder. "Great. Here comes the food! I'm starving!" The dinner was wonderful and, as we ate, we continued to flirt with each other. She enjoyed laughing more than anyone I had ever met. But it was her intensity and passion that really attracted me. She shared her deepest feelings, her innermost thoughts, in a way that made me feel very special.

By the time we got to dessert, those feelings began to surface. "You know," she said, "I love you in a way I never expected to love anyone. It's a beautiful feeling -- much like a bouquet of delicate flowers. I feel such joy from sharing something so special as you. I trust that I can be myself with you and I'm thankful that I allowed myself to be vulnerable enough to open myself up to love you."

"I'm thankful too. I wouldn't have missed this experience for anything. I love you, Kathy. You're the most important person in my world. You've made my life so beautiful. I can't imagine being without you. I want so much to make you happy."

She just looked at me for what seemed like several minutes. Then she said, "Let's go. I want to be alone with you."

"You don't have to ask me twice," I said standing up. We raced home in record time.

When we got to her door, she paused. "I'm going to miss coming home with you. It's really been so wonderful having you here." Once inside, she pulled me close and whispered, "I want to show you how much I love you."

"You do that in so many ways. More than you know."

We walked up the stairs. "I'm going to take a bath. Want to come with?" "My, my. You have such good ideas tonight."

"Give me a few minutes to get things ready."

As she walked to her bedroom, I went downstairs, took off my clothes and put on a robe. When I got back, she was in the bathroom. She called out, "One more minute." When she called me in, she was laying neck-deep in bubbles. Her hair was pinned up on top of her head. She smiled and said, "Come on in. I'll make room for you." She sat up, pulling the bubbles above her breasts. I took off my robe and started getting in by her feet. "No. Turn around and lean against me." She spread her legs and I wiggled between them. I leaned my head back just above her breasts. "Comfy?"

"Very," I answered softly.

"Mmmm. I could stay like this all night," she murmured. She took a handful of bubbles and gently rubbed them down my arms. Then she cupped both of my breasts and caressed them softly. The water on her fingertips made her touch even more sensual and I became aroused easily. My nipples hardened as she made little circular motions around them with the bubbles. Finally, when I couldn't stand it anymore, I put my hands on top of hers and pressed them against me. She rubbed both of my nipples at the same time now, rolling them between her finger and thumb. "You're driving me crazy, you know."

"Turn around so I can kiss you," she said in a voice that was so urgent, I barely recognized it.

I pulled away so I could turn my body around and scooted up so that my legs were on each side of her and I could reach her lips with mine. Our lips were wet and soft from the water, but our tongues were hot as they met with a passion I had rarely felt. I reached for her breasts and caressed them with water as she had done to me. I tried to push closer, but couldn't. "Let's get out." We stood up together, with our mouths still locked together. I reached for a towel and wrapped it around her and started patting her dry. Then, I moved my mouth down to her breast as I put my hand between her legs. Her legs were shaking so she leaned against the wall. I knelt before her and kissed the top of her thighs. When I moved my mouth between them, she put both of her hands on my head and spread her legs further apart. I ran my tongue up and down her outer lips. She pushed my head closer as I penetrated deeper. She moaned my name over and over. "Susan, don't stop. Please, don't stop." I put my hands behind her and pulled her even closer applying more pressure with my tongue. When I felt her climax starting, I continued to lick her as she shook uncontrollably above me. "Oh my God, my God," she murmured. When she stopped shaking, I lifted my head and looked up at her. "Susan, my legs are like rubber. I never knew I could feel like this."

I helped her to the bed and then snuggled up beside her. "It wasn't supposed to happen this way."

"What do you mean?" I was puzzled. I thought the experience was just beautiful!

"I wanted to make love to you."

I smiled. "Just let me just hold you for a while. We have plenty of time for everything."

I had fallen asleep, but awoke to her touch. She had positioned herself so that she was kneeling above me, her legs straddling my thighs. She leaned forward and started kissing my neck. She moved her mouth down to my shoulder and trailed little kisses down to my breast. She took it in her mouth and ran her tongue over my nipple. I tried to touch her, but she pushed my hand away, whispering, "Let me make love to you. I just want you to enjoy it." Her mouth left my breast and started trailing soft, little kisses down my body as she stretched her legs out between mine. Her kisses continued downward and stopped at my navel, putting her tongue inside and licking it in a circular motion. I tried to press against her, but she moved her body away. She continued her journey with her mouth and tongue until at last she reached my groin. Her face was between my legs. I could hardly breathe. She started kissing my inner thighs, and, when she sensed I couldn't stand it any longer, she started softly licking me. I pressed myself against her mouth, moaning with pleasure. Ever so softly she licked me in my most sensitive spots. She moved her hands up to my breasts and rubbed both nipples with her thumbs. My body started moving involuntarily as I pressed even closer to her touch, and I could feel my orgasm starting to rise from deep within. Then she moved her tongue faster and harder and I felt like I was going to explode. I strained to meet her mouth as my body began to shake uncontrollably. I was totally consumed by her love.

When I was still, she pulled herself up to face me again. "I loved that. Did you like it?"

"A little," I teased.

"That was my secret surprise. You nearly ruined it." "You were right. It's my new favorite thing to do."

"I've been wanting to do that ever since the night we first went up on the hill."

"So, why did you wait so long?" "I was afraid," she whispered. "Of what?"

"That I'd fall hopelessly in love with you." "Are you still afraid?"

"Yes, but not because of that anymore. I'm already in love with you." "What then?"

"I'm afraid I'll never have the strength to leave." At the time I thought it was an odd thing to say. Another warning sign I just ignored.

"Maybe you won't ever want to," I said hopefully.

"Maybe. I know right now I couldn't even think of it. I'm content and I'm happy. I want to share everything with you."

"Would you ever consider moving in with me?" I regretted asking as soon as I said it. I knew it was much too early in our relationship to consider it, even though I fantasized about it almost from the beginning. She kept it light. "You mean with you and Lynn?"

"No silly. We'd find our own place." "So, what would I tell John?"

"Would he believe that we're good friends and you want to be roomies with me?"

"I'll think of something. Just try to be patient." "Can I ask you something?"

"You can ask anything. It doesn't mean I'll answer."

"Why do you live with him? You have to admit it's kind of unusual."

She laughed. "It was my father's doing actually. After we both ended up here, he suggested that we buy a house together for an investment. And it was a good idea. It's appreciated a lot since we bought it a couple of years ago."

"But what if one of you met someone else you wanted to live with?"

"We've already discussed that. We made an agreement that whoever gets married first gets the house and will buy the other one out."

"Does he have a girlfriend? Maybe I can fix him up." "Now. Now." "You know I'm kidding. Sort of."

"Look, honey. Let's just take it day by day for a while."

I hugged her and pulled her close. "I just don't want to leave you." "I know. This can't be settled now. But I know what can be."

"What?" She kissed me. And for a while, I forgot about everything else.

CHAPTER ELEVEN

I WAS UNPACKING MY CLOTHES WHEN Lynn walked in. "Hello stranger. Welcome home. Did you have a good time?"

"I had an unbelievable time. How 'bout you? What have you been up to?" "If you were really interested you could have called once or twice," she said sarcastically.

"I thought about it. But truthfully, I know that you disapprove and I just didn't want any negativity."

"How many times do I have to tell you this. I don't disapprove. I just think you're going to end up getting hurt and I would hate to see that happen."

"I don't really care. I don't care about anything these days, except my life with her."

"Yeah. You're sure making that real clear. You know, if that's how you feel, why don't you just live with her?"

"I would, and I hope to, but it can't happen now." I didn't want to tell her too much about my hopes and plans. It was private between me and Kathy.

"Well, I don't think it will ever happen." "Why are you so angry?"

"Look, we were good friends before you met her and now you hardly give me the time of day. How do you think that makes me feel?" She was right. I hardly saw her anymore.

"Oh Lynn. I'm sorry. I wasn't thinking. You're always so busy dating that I really didn't think it mattered to you."

"Well, it does Susan. I'm really hurt." I was surprised, then

73

embarrassed that I hadn't even considered her feelings.

"I said I was sorry. Really I am. Hey, how 'bout going out to dinner. We haven't done anything together in ages."

"That's my point."

"And you've made it several times now. I get it already. What else can I do?"

"You can show some interest in my life."

"Of course. I've really treated you badly. It wasn't intentional. So really, what have you been doing?"

"Bill and I broke up. I've just been hanging out here."

"Oh, so that's it. You should have called me. You could have come out with us."

"I didn't want to interfere. I've really missed you, you jerk."

She came over and gave me a big hug. I forgot how vulnerable and sensitive she could be. It had been a long time since she shared her feelings with me.

"I'm really sorry I've been neglecting you. Come on, let's get something to eat."

"Give me a few minutes to change."

"So, what's so special about her?" she asked when we got to the restaurant. "Everything."

"Like what?"

"Well, she's supportive and encouraging. She's sexy and passionate. And she's more vulnerable and open than anyone I've ever met. I love her depth and insight. But most of all, she makes me feel like I'm the most important person in the world."

She looked sad. "What's wrong?"

"I think I've lost you to her. I didn't realize this until you were gone, but my feelings for you run a lot deeper than I thought."

"What are you saying?"

"Is it too late to have a second chance with you?" I was dumbfounded.

"Did I miss something?"

"I'm asking if you could have feelings for me again." "Are you saying that you want us to be involved?" "Yes." I was shocked!

"But I think you just want me because I'm not available anymore. If I said yes, you'd probably faint."

"Try me."

"Look, I've watched you with men. You love the chase but once you hook them, you're not interested anymore. It would be the same with me."

"Are you psychoanalyzing me now?" She was annoyed.

"No. I'm just telling you the truth. Come on, you know it's true." "Then why do I feel so jealous?"

"Look, you've known me for almost three years. Why now, after all this time?"

"I just think I took it for granted that you'd always be there."

"Yes, and when I was, you never thought seriously of having a relationship with me, right?"

"But I never realized how much I depended on you. Like I said, you were just always there."

"Lynn, I'll still be there as a friend. I'll always love you. But not in the same way I love Kathy. I don't think I'll ever love anyone else the way I love her." I paused. "Come on, don't be sad. Actually, I'd like you to get to know her. I want you to be part of our lives."

"You're talking like you have a future with her."

"I want to believe that. I do believe it when we're together." "Well, if it doesn't work out, maybe..."

I stopped her before she could finish her sentence. "There is no maybe with us. We had our time and now it's over. We can't go back there again."

"We wouldn't be going back. We'd be going forward."

I laughed. "I'll bet in two weeks you'll be madly in love with some guy and you'll forget all about this conversation."

She smiled. "I may be dating someone, but I won't forget this conversation. Nor will you."

"Ok. Ok. Let's order. I'm really hungry."

The phone was ringing as we got back to the apartment. It was Kathy. "Where have you been? I've been calling you for hours."

"Lynn and I went out for dinner. How are you? I miss you."

"I'm fine and I miss you too. So, did Lynn miss you? I'm worried that she'll want you back."

"Don't be silly," I lied. "That was over a long time ago. Besides, she knows I'm madly in love with you. How's John?"

"He caught a lot of fish and, guess what! He's met someone he really likes." "Really. How exciting!"

She laughed. "I thought you'd like that news."

"You bet. I hope he wants to be with her every night, so that I can be with you."

"Well, don't worry. We'll see each other a lot." "I love you, Kathy."

"And I love you. Sweet dreams." "See you at work. Goodnight."

I felt guilty for lying to her about Lynn. But I wanted to protect her from feeling pain. I think it was the first and last time I ever succeeded.

After saying goodnight to Lynn, I went to my room to finish unpacking. At the bottom of my suitcase, there was an envelope with my name on it. It was Kathy's handwriting. I went to my bed and opened it.

My dearest Susan:

How often I have thought or even started to write to you on paper the thoughts and feelings I have inside. And now, I'm facing sharing for these moments those innermost feelings of love, joy, companionship, and excitement; all the feelings we have together that make us both real.

When we first struggled to voice our feelings of love, I can remember the queasiness inside and the awkwardness outside. I remember the surge of energy that went through my body as it still does when the awareness of our true love is actualized. I know that it's special to express and share together our feelings. No one can take that away -- I'm so glad. What we experienced is ours together, never to be given away or abused by someone else.

And yet, with the excitement of loving you comes deep pain and guilt. I want so much to share openly and with love whenever I'm around you, but I don't feel I can. I feel guilt as if I've done something wrong, yet it's so innocent. I'm wrapped up in you and it feels so good to share our love -- why must it be considered bad?

So, if you see me pull away, it's not because of less love or loss of something precious. It's confusion and a feeble attempt on my part not to feel guilt from our behavior.

But right now, I feel deep, intense love -- deep, yet noticeably blue in hue. I feel like the first plants in the garden breaking ground only to find there were other plants I could not see, underground, who were also breaking ground. I'm describing hope -- hope that all may someday find the type of total love -- of joy, acceptance, peace, and thankfulness I feel with you.

All my love, Kathy

I fell asleep holding her letter to my heart.

CHAPTER TWELVE

THINGS WENT VERY SMOOTHLY THE next several weeks. Teresa adjusted well at Doug and Mary's house. I saw her every week. She rarely talked about her parents and focused more on her new friends at school or about how excited she was when Mary took her shopping to buy new clothes. She started wearing lipstick and was learning how to dance. She loved to eat junk food, talk to her girlfriends on the phone and listen to her favorite songs on the radio. She was turning into a real teenager! Doug and Mary were very affectionate with her. She loved the attention. Though her parents resisted every step of the way, they did manage to attend several family sessions. It was very painful for Teresa, especially when they finally told her that Ed was not her father. But Doug and Mary were so loving and supportive that she recovered quickly; outwardly, at least. I put the word out to the adoption workers to look for a couple that might consider taking a thirteen-year-old, as it became more and more obvious to me that her parents did not want her back. That was okay with me. Kathy kept telling me that a social worker has to maintain an unbiased perception, but I couldn't help believing that Teresa was better off without them. Though I couldn't prove it, I had a strong feeling that Ed, and possibly even Patsy, had been physically abusive toward her.

The rest of the program was also going well. We had placed a total of nine children in seven different foster homes, and I was very busy with interviews, home visits and family sessions.

The women's group continued to thrive. The support they gave to each other was always an uplifting part of the week. They shared their inner feelings about their families, their husbands and boyfriends, and their children. They laughed and cried together. They cheered each other's successes and helped each other gain strength from their failures. Mostly, they gave each other hope. I felt honored to be part of it.

Lynn began dating a new beau and was back to her old self. "This time I'm really in love, Susan. He's just the most wonderful man I've ever met." I just smiled, even though in the back of my mind I thought, "Here we go again."

John's relationship was progressing. He saw his new girlfriend about two times a week and shared with Kathy that "Things are getting pretty serious." I had my fingers crossed.

But, by far, the best part of my life was the time I spent with Kathy. Each day we got closer and shared more of ourselves with each other. She continued to be very supportive at work, but as I became more proficient at my job, I could be more independent and saw her less there. At the end of each day, we would get together in her office so that I could bring her up to date on what was happening with all of my clients. She really enjoyed seeing me get excited with the progress they were making and would laugh as I told her funny stories about the foster parents and kids. One day I came into her office still giggling over going into one home and seeing a five-year-old boy walking around in his foster mother's high heels.

Sometimes we'd have dinner together and then snuggle in the back seat of her car. We'd have to find a dark street even though I kept telling her that we could go back to my apartment. But she still felt hesitant about being affectionate around other people.

"But we'd go in my room. I could lock the door." "She'd know what we were doing."

I'd laugh and just hug her. I didn't want to push too much.

We had wonderful conversations in that Bug. We talked about

what we were like as kids.

"I'm glad I didn't meet you back then, Susan. I don't think you would have liked me. I was really shy and spent most of the time in my room reading Nancy Drew mysteries."

"You probably wouldn't have liked me either. I was a real tomboy. All I wanted to do with my summers was play baseball with the neighborhood boys. I got pretty good at it too. When I was in junior high school, I joined a girl's softball league. Mom and Annie would come to every game and scream and yell, even if I struck out, which I did quite often. I loved those summers. I didn't have a care in the world."

"I like baseball. If I knew you, I would have come to the games," she said pulling me closer. "I'll bet you looked so cute in your little uniform."

"Well, I still have it. Maybe we can play catch sometime." I didn't wait for an answer. I just kissed her.

Occasionally she would try to explain to me why she didn't think her family would accept her being involved with a woman. "They're even more religious than I am, Susan. According to the Bible, it's a sin." I tried to understand, but it was like she was speaking a foreign language. How could something so beautiful be wrong? I really had my head in the sand when she talked about religion. It would be a long time before I realized what a serious issue it was to her. Sometimes I wondered how my parents would have felt about my being gay. I finally decided that it wouldn't have been a big deal. After all, I was the middle child!

One night she surprised me. "My sister called today. She'll be here next Friday." We were holding hands in the back of her car. "I've decided I'm going to tell her about you."

"Oh, Kathy. Are you sure?"

"I feel closer to her than anyone else besides you. We've shared a lot of secrets together. Even if she doesn't approve, I know she won't tell the rest of my family. Do you want to meet her while she's here?"

"Only if I can meet her before you tell her," I joked. "Ha. Ha. I never knew you were such a chicken."

"I never knew I was either." We both laughed. I kissed her then and she responded passionately. "Come home with me. Spend the night. You can't imagine how much I miss holding you."

"Yes I can," she whispered. "It gets harder and harder for me to leave you." "Then don't. You can call John from my apartment. You can tell him you

had a few drinks and you don't feel safe driving home. Lynn went out with her new boyfriend. She might not even come home tonight. Come on, say yes."

"Yes."

"Oh my God, really? Really?" I was ecstatic. Just the thought of being in bed with her again aroused me.

"Yes."

"Let's go then."

She had never been to my apartment. When I opened the door, she looked around, smiling. "It's just like I pictured it. Is that where you call me from?" she said pointing to the phone in the kitchen.

"No. I have a phone in my room. I'm usually lying in my bed. Come on, I'll show you."

I led her to my bedroom, then scribbled a quick note to Lynn and taped it to my door while Kathy called John. It read: "Don't come in. I have a guest."

"I think his girlfriend was there," she said hanging up. "He didn't mind at all. He said you should take good care of me." She had a wicked smile on her face.

"You bet I will." I walked over to her and slowly began unbuttoning her blouse. When I had finished, she held her arms out, so I could slip it off easily. Then she kicked off her loafers. I unbuttoned her pants and pulled down the zipper. Then I pulled them down over her hips and helped her step out of each leg. Next I unhooked her bra. She stood there, in her panties, just waiting. I almost forgot how beautiful she was. I pulled back the covers and helped her into bed. As she laid there, I slowly began to strip. She watched every move. "What a wonderful treat" she said as I got down to my panties. I teased her by pulling them down very, very slowly. I got into bed and held her close. We didn't sleep the rest of the night.

I was early. I tried to do some work as I waited, but I was too nervous to concentrate. We decided to meet at the beach, and then walk out to the end of the pier for lunch. I saw them pull into the parking lot. I was relieved to see that they were both smiling. Jenny was about three inches taller than Kathy. Her hair was black and she wore it short and curly. Her face was full and round, with big green eyes, and thick, red lips. Though she was pretty, they didn't look at all like sisters. Kathy was much softer and more feminine-looking.

Kathy waved when she saw me. I walked to meet them and was pleasantly surprised when she gave me a quick hug. "Hi, Susan. This is my sister, Jenny." I shook her hand and we exchanged smiles.

"Are you guys hungry or do you want to walk on the beach for a while." "I'm starving," Jenny said. "Let's eat first." Kathy was in the middle as we walked and every so often her hand brushed against mine. I knew it wasn't an accident. Jenny talked about how beautiful the ocean was and what a good time they'd been having since she got here four days ago. They went to Disneyland, Hollywood and the San Diego Zoo. "I think I liked Hollywood, the best. I loved looking at the footprints of the stars. It's just so glamorous."

We were seated at a booth, Jenny and Kathy on one side and me on the other. I tried not to look at Kathy for fear that Jenny would notice the love in my eyes. "So, Kathy told me you work together," she said as she looked at the menu.

"It's more than that. Your sister hired me when I was giving up hope of ever finding a job. And she's been a wonderful supervisor."

"You're really good friends too."

"Yes, very good friends." Kathy smiled.

Just then, two women walked into the restaurant. One was very masculine-looking and obviously gay. When they sat down, they sat on the same side of the booth and discreetly held hands.

"Boy, you'd never see that in Kansas," Jenny whispered. "I've never seen dykes hold hands in public before. I just don't get two women together, do you?"

"To each his own I always say," I answered casually, trying to hide how uncomfortable I was feeling.

Kathy looked really shaken. "You know Jenny...," she hesitated. I held my breath. Don't tell her now, I thought. "I have a good friend that's gay and she's really a wonderful person. I enjoy spending time with her. And I like her girlfriend a lot too."

"Really? I've never known anyone that's gay."

"You might be surprised. A lot of gay women don't look like her," Kathy said, glancing at the booth where they sat. "And most women wouldn't tell you if they thought you'd feel negative about it."

"I think I could tell if someone was gay, Kathy," Jenny answered sarcastically.

"Well, what are you guys going to order?" I didn't like how this was going at all.

Jenny decided right away. Kathy was still upset. I slipped off my sandal and touched her with my toes under the table. She jumped a little, until she realized what was happening. She looked at me as though she was asking a question. I looked back shaking my head no as Jenny eyed the lesbians across the room. She understood. This just wasn't the right time to tell her about us.

"So, what do you want to do after lunch, Jenny? There are some real unique shops on Main Street. Want to do a little shopping?"

"Oh, Kathy, you know I'd love that. It's one of my favorite things to do. Maybe we can shop today and do your favorite thing tomorrow."

I'll never know how she kept a straight face. "Oh, that's okay, Jen. This is your week. I want to spoil you."

I changed the subject. "So, how do you like your brother's new girlfriend?" "She's real nice. I'd like to meet Kathy's boyfriend, but she's hiding him from me."

"I didn't know you had a boyfriend, Kath," I said, trying to sound casual. "Oh, she'll deny it. But I can always tell when she's in love. She just looks so happy."

"I told you, Jenny, I am happy. But I don't have a boyfriend." She was beginning to get a little irritated.

"I don't believe you. But that's okay. You're probably afraid I'll steal him away like I did in high school. What was that guy's name?"

"David."

"Yeah, David. You remember, don't you?"

"He was hardly my boyfriend. I had just been out with him a few times." "Yeah, but you were real upset when he called and asked me out."

"I wasn't upset about him calling. I was upset that you said yes."

"I know. That was so mean. What an idiot I was. I would never do that now."

"Jenny, I really don't have a boyfriend," she laughed.

"Remember how you used to talk about getting married when you were young so that you could have lots of children. Do you still want children?"

"Of course I do." Kathy seemed to avoid looking at me when she answered. "Well, you'd better get busy and find a husband. Time is slipping by, you know."

I was feeling more uncomfortable every minute, but there was no escape. I just ate my lunch quietly and tried to appear interested in their conversation. But Jenny was starting to get on my nerves. I wouldn't tell Kathy, but I really didn't like her.

"Do you have a boyfriend, Susan?" "No. Not right now. Do you?"

"Yes. We've been going together for a long time. We're planning to get married next year. Maybe you can come out with Kathy for the wedding."

"I'd love that," I said, trying to sound excited.

As we were walking back, Kathy asked me to go shopping with them, but I politely begged off, saying I had a lot of errands to do. The truth was, I couldn't wait to get away from them. I didn't want to hear about old boyfriends, getting married, and having children. I wanted to tell Jenny, "Look, your sister loves me. I make her happy. Not some boyfriend!" but, of course, I couldn't. I just said a polite goodbye. "Have a good trip home, Jenny. It was great to meet you."

The tears started flowing before I even reached my car.

I didn't hear from Kathy the rest of the day, nor the next. That old scary feeling was in the pit of my stomach. I prayed that Kathy didn't tell her sister about us. I felt that Jenny wouldn't approve and would try to influence Kathy to break it off. She finally called the next morning.

"Susan, I felt so bad about what happened at lunch. Are you okay? You left in such a hurry. I was worried about you."

"You were worried about me? I saw the look on your face. You looked devastated."

"I was shocked. I never heard her talk like that before." "You didn't tell her about us, did you?"

"How could I? But it really made me sad. I'm tired of all these lies. Is this the way it's always going to be?"

"Of course not." I tried to reassure her, but I wasn't really sure myself. This was new for me too.

"It's so hard for me sometimes. I'm just not used to it."

"I know. It's hard for me too. I just want to tell the world how wonderful you are and how much I love you. I think there are a lot of people that would be happy for us."

"At least you live with someone who knows. I have to lie to John almost every day. It's getting so difficult for me to be here." I felt selfish. I didn't think a lot about how hard it was for her. I just thought about how good it felt for me.

"I hate that you're having such a difficult time. You know, I cried all the way home. I'm afraid that reality is setting in and you'll decide you don't want to be with me."

"I love you. You know that. But I am starting to realize how much I have to give up to be with you. This is so much more complicated than I could have ever predicted."

"And that's what scares me."

"But you give up a lot too. Don't you hate the sneaking around and lying to everyone?"

"Yes. But I never doubt that you're worth it."

"I'm sorry. I didn't mean to imply that you're not. I'm not confused about the way I feel about you. I'm just confused about how to handle it with the rest of the world."

"Maybe you think about it too much. Can't we just enjoy what we have. People will think what they want to. We can't change that."

"But I care about some of those people very much."

"And they'll care about you, no matter who you choose to be with." Even as I said it, I wasn't sure it was true.

"I wish I had your confidence."

I tried to lighten things up. "Don't you think I could win them over? I'd just turn on the charm with your parents and they'd be begging you to get involved with me."

She laughed. "You're a very weird person. But I'm sure you know that." "And you're crazy about me, right?"

"Right. Let's have dinner tomorrow after work."

"As long as we don't go back to that restaurant where those dykes were. You know how I feel about that," I teased.

"You are too much. You're seriously disturbed. But I love you." "I love you too."

When we hung up, I thought about what she said. I knew she was really struggling and I felt bad about that. I didn't want our relationship to cause her any unhappiness. But I didn't want her to leave me either. She was right about one thing. The relationship was getting very complicated. And I knew she thought about the complications a lot more than I did. That's what scared me so much.

CHAPTER THIRTEEN

NOW THAT ALL OF OUR foster homes were filled with kids, I spent the majority of my time visiting and getting to know them. I was fond of all of them, but my favorite was a ten-year-old boy named Joey. His mother was a drug addict and she would leave him alone for days at a time, while she went on a binge. The neighbors would report it, and Joey would be picked up. Then his mother would manage to stay clean for a few weeks, so that she could get him back. But she couldn't stay off drugs for long and Joey would end up alone again. The third time she got him back, she was warned that this would be her last chance. If she started using again, he would be placed in long-term foster care. It didn't take long for that to happen. That's when we stepped in.

Joey was a street-wise, mischievous, precocious boy. He was small for his age, with a crew cut, chubby cheeks and bright blue eyes. He looked more like six or seven, so his wisecracks and command of the language surprised people when they first talked to him. He was good at manipulating to get what he wanted and could have a naive adult wrapped around his finger in five minutes flat. He was the kind of kid people either loved or hated. I fell into the first category.

We connected right away. He was very angry. I made him laugh. He was frightened. I calmed him down. He felt abandoned. I gave him hope. When I dropped him off at his new home, I promised to visit him twice a week. I never broke that promise. After a few months, he knew that he could trust and confide in me. He knew I was his friend.

I usually saved my visit with him for last, so we could spend extra time together. Since his mother and father were Hispanic, I had placed him in our only Hispanic foster home. The foster parents, Mr. and Mrs. Gonzales, had two of their own children, but wanted a larger family. When Socorro found out she couldn't have more children, they decided to become foster parents. She loved being a homemaker. Her husband, Manuel, worked very long hours as a plumber, but he always spent time with the children when he came home, no matter how tired he was. They did very well in our training program. I liked them both very much and had no hesitation about placing children in their home.

Joey answered the door when I knocked.

He smiled when he saw me. "Susan, you look beautiful today."

"I'm not letting you go home yet, Joey. So you can cut the flattery." I could talk to him like that. In fact, he liked it. "So what mischief have you gotten yourself into lately?"

"Hi Socorro. How's our little guy today?" I asked, as I gave him a hug.

"I don't know where he learns some of the words he says. We don't like our children to hear bad words. When he swears, we make him go to his room." Socorro seemed genuinely concerned.

"Does it help?"

"Hell no," Joey piped in.

"Come on, Joey. I think we need to have a long talk. Let's go for a walk." "Oh goody," he said sarcastically and put his hand in mine.

"Aren't you a little old to hold my hand, pal?"

"Gee Susan, I thought you'd think I was too young for you."

I couldn't help but laugh. "Okay. You can hold my hand, but don't try anything else."

When we got outside, he was suddenly serious. "My mom called me yesterday."

"How's she doing?"

"I think she's really trying. She says she misses me and wants me back." "I'm sure she means that. But she needs help, Joey. And she's not going to get better until she gets serious about getting that help."

There were tears in his eyes. "I know she's going to get better, Susan. I'm real important to her."

"You know, Joey. You're really special to me too." I meant that. I'd never met a child that, in many ways, was more grown up than I was. I always knew where I stood with Joey. If he trusted you, he would be open and honest when expressing his feelings.

"I am?" He was genuinely surprised.

"Yes. I think you're a great kid. How are things with Socorro and Manuel?" "They're okay. The kids are really sissies though. They're always afraid

they're going to get in trouble. It's boring." Javier was nine and Maria was six. Both of them were very shy and quiet-- the complete opposite of Joey.

"And why would they think they were going to get in trouble?" "Uh oh. I slipped, didn't I?"

"Joey, what have you been up to?"

"I just wanted them to sneak into the movies with me. But they wouldn't do it."

"Look, I want you to be a good influence on these kids. You have to set an example. Sometimes I don't think your mom set a good example for you."

"Why would you say that?" he snapped back at me. "She never tried to sneak into the movies." I knew he was serious, so I kept my smile to myself.

"You're right. I shouldn't have said that about your mother. I'm sorry." But I knew he got the point. So did I. He was fiercely protective of his mother.

"Okay. I forgive you." He seemed to relish this little victory. I'm sure he didn't feel like he won many battles in his life. He deserved one every once in a while.

"How 'bout some ice cream?"

"I'd rather have a hamburger. I haven't had one since I moved in here." "OK. A hamburger it is. Let's go."

Kathy was waiting for me when I got back. We hadn't seen much of each other since her sister left. "I have good news for you. You're finally getting your own office. In fact, it will be right next to mine."

"How did you swing that?"

"Well, I have to admit, I didn't really have anything to do with it. Connie gave her notice today. She'll be leaving next week."

"That's great," I said coolly, barely looking at her.

"Have you got any plans for dinner? I feel like we haven't talked in a long time."

"Yeah. I promised Lynn I'd go out with her and Dennis tonight. I think they may be getting engaged."

"Really? That's fast."

"I don't know for sure. But she spends all of her time with him. Maybe heterosexual relationships are less complicated." I tried not to be sarcastic.

She paused. "Susan, what's wrong? You've just been so distant lately." "Kath, I know you're having a lot of reservations about this relationship. I'm just trying to give you some space, but every time I see you I wonder, is this the day she'll tell me she doesn't want to see me anymore? Is this the day she'll tell me it was all a mistake? I'm just really frightened. I don't want to lose you."

"Susan, there are no guarantees about anything in this world. I want to be with you now. You keep telling me to just take it one day at a time. I'm really trying hard to do that."

"And now look at me, not practicing what I preach. I hate feeling this way." "I never pegged you for a pessimist. I thought I was the one who had all the doubts."

"Maybe it's catching."

"Boy, you really are in a funk."

I wasn't in a funk but I needed some reassurance and I couldn't ask for it. I wanted her to give it to me freely on her own. "Oh, don't mind me. I'll snap out of it. How was your day?"

"Oh my God. I nearly forgot. Mindy thinks she may have found someone that's interested in adopting Teresa. She's going to tell us all about it in the staff meeting tomorrow morning."

"Great. I really have to go, Kath." "Okay. I'll see you tomorrow."

Lynn and Dennis were sitting in the bar waiting for me. "Sorry I'm late. What's up?"

"We have great news, Susan. Can we get you a drink?" I ordered a Scotch. "Dennis and I are getting married."

I tried to act surprised. "That's great." I hugged them both at once. "When?" "In three weeks."

"Three weeks! What's the rush?"

"Susan, I'm pregnant." Then she quickly added, "We were going to get married anyway. We're just moving it up a little. So, will you be my maid of honor?" At least I never had to worry about getting pregnant. God knows I had enough to worry about.

"Of course. Where are you guys going to live?"

"At my place in the beginning." Dennis chimed in. "We hope to buy our own home in a year or two."

"This way we figure you won't have to move if you don't want to. You can get another roommate to help with the rent," Lynn added. I wondered if she was being sarcastic.

"Great!" I wanted to cry. Was I going to lose both Lynn and Kathy at the same time?

"It's not going to be a big wedding, but I'm going to wear a traditional dress. Will you help me shop? We'll find a dress for you too."

"Yes. I'll help in any way I can."

"You're such a good friend; you really are."

I wondered if she ever thought about our conversation, what, two months ago? How quickly things can change. I was right about her finding someone else. I just hoped she wasn't right about how things would go with Kathy.

The staff meeting was scheduled for 9:00.

"We're all anxious to hear about the possible parents for Teresa," Kathy said.

"Well, actually, it's a parent," Mindy began. "Betty is a thirty-eight year-old woman who's never been married, but wants a child. She comes from a large family who are supportive of her in this decision. She has a Master's Degree in business and has a good job with IBM. She's very active in the community doing volunteer work for local hospitals and charities. She told me she has a very full, satisfying life and she'd like to share it with a child. She's been trying to adopt through the County for three years. In that time, they called her with one opportunity, but she felt it wasn't a good match."

"Why? What were the circumstances?" I asked.

"Well, I don't have all of the details, but the child had a lot of medical problems and she just felt she was ill equipped to handle it. After that, they didn't call her again. They denied they were holding that against her, but she was feeling pretty hopeless about getting another chance with them. I have a friend that works for the county and she suggested to Betty that she call us. They've already done the investigation on her. She has a clean record."

"And she doesn't feel that a thirteen-year-old child is too old?" I was skeptical.

"Apparently she's thinking seriously about it. She wants to meet Teresa."

I thought Teresa was better off with Doug and Mary than her own parents. She was really happy there and was starting to feel good about herself. I wasn't sure this was the best time to move her. In fact, I didn't want to move her at all. "Well, doesn't Teresa get a say in all of this. She's just adjusted to being at Doug and Mary's and now we're going to move her again?" I was upset. I didn't want Teresa to keep losing the people she loved -- like I did.

"Susan, that's where you come in. Of course she has a say in it. And she'll have a chance to say a final goodbye to her family. You'll be with her every step of the way to help her process everything." Kathy was trying to be positive, but she didn't understand. After all, her family was still intact.

I turned to Mindy. "Well, what's the next step?"

"I think you should meet with Betty so that you can give her more information about Teresa. And, if she wants to go forward, then you can tell her family that you may have found a permanent home. If they're willing to give her up, then we'll arrange a meeting between Betty and Teresa." Mindy had it all worked out.

I tried to look happy, but I wasn't. Everything was changing too fast for me. I felt overwhelmed. When the meeting was over, Kathy led me to her office.

"Susan, I thought this is what you wanted for Teresa."

I didn't want to argue with her. I knew it wouldn't change anything. "I know. I don't know what's wrong with me lately. I just seem to blow everything out of proportion." I wanted to be more open with her, but I just couldn't. I felt too fragile. I was so afraid I was losing her.

"What happened with Lynn yesterday?"

"She's getting married and moving in with Dennis at the end of the month." "Wow. So, you were right. What are you going to do?"

"I don't know yet. I'll probably just stay where I am until I figure it out. Can we have dinner later?" I asked hopefully.

"I wish I could, but I told John I'd go out to dinner with him and Ann tonight. He wants me to get to know her better." I felt angry. Why doesn't she say it! She just doesn't want to spend time with me.

"Okay then." I got up to leave, but Kathy stopped me.

"Susan, shut the door." Afterwards, she said, "Are you okay? I hate to see you so unhappy."

"You know, ever since your sister was here, I just feel like we're drifting further apart. And I don't know how to stop it. I guess I'm expecting the worst."

"You're right, Susan. I won't lie to you. I'm questioning a lot of things. I'm just very confused. I'm sure of one thing though. I don't want to hurt you."

"I know you don't. And I don't want you to feel like you have to give up a lot of things to be with me."

"Susan, everything is a choice. That's what life is about. Everyone has to give up things for any relationship, whether they know it or not. It's a serious decision."

"Not for me. I mean, it's serious, but it's easy. I want to be with you. That's the most important thing to me. What's to think about?" It sounded so superficial, but it was true.

"There are a lot of other things to consider. I can't believe you don't know that."

"Sometimes I feel like I'm asking too much of you to love me."

She raised her voice. "Oh no! It has nothing to do with loving you. Is that what you think we're talking about?"

"Aren't we?" I started to feel very anxious.

"Look, we're talking about a whole different way of life. Are you really prepared to live a gay lifestyle? Do you even know what that would be like?" I was stunned. She was right. I never thought about it. I never really had to. My decisions didn't affect anyone but me. I didn't have a family to consider and my best friend was already very supportive. I never worried about the religious issues. I just didn't believe that God would punish people for loving each other. The only thing I worried about was Kathy leaving me. What an airhead! "Now

I feel like a real idiot!"

"You're not an idiot. You're the person I love. I'm not confused about that. Look, I have an appointment and have to go. Can we talk again tomorrow?"

"Yes. Dinner?" She shook her head and gave me a quick kiss. For the first time in weeks, I was able to breathe easier.

I spent the rest of the day moving into my new office. I did a good job of pretending I would miss being in the same room with the adoption workers. "But I'm just going to be down the hall," I said to Mindy as she moped around watching me gather up my things.

"We're happy for you that you're getting your own office, but you were so pleasant to have in here. Now we'll have to get adjusted to someone new."

"Oh Mindy. It will be okay." I tried to sound sympathetic but it was difficult not to smile.

The first interview I had in my new office was with Betty. I found her to be a very warm and intelligent woman, who seemed to have a good sense of who she was and what she wanted. She was the oldest of nine children and was given a lot of responsibility for watching and caring for her younger brothers and sisters. She was sixteen when the last one was born, so "I practically raised her myself." She had no reservations about her parenting skills and felt she had a lot to offer a child both emotionally and financially. She liked her job and made a good salary. She had a wonderful sense of humor and seemed at ease talking to people. She admitted she had some concerns about taking a thirteen-year-old "but," she joked, "I can keep my name on the list for a younger child and, if I'm lucky enough to get one, Teresa will be old enough to help."

She asked a lot of appropriate questions about Teresa and her family. When she finished, I shifted gears. "I know this is a really personal question Betty, but I'm just curious. Is there a reason you never married?"

"No reason in particular. I guess I never met the right man. I've always wanted children and, at one point in my life, was almost desperate to find a husband. But when I realized that I could have a child without having a husband, I changed my priorities. That's when I contacted the County Adoption Agency."

"I know you've done a background check with them, but you're probably going to have to go through it again with us. We're not going to find any deep dark secrets, are we?" I asked smiling.

"Everyone has a dark secret or two, but my records are clean."

"And you're absolutely sure that Teresa isn't too old for you?" I wanted to be sure this would be Teresa's last move.

"Absolutely."

I liked her a lot, but I had a feeling that she was hiding something. For the time being, I kept it to myself. But I was pretty sure that Betty was gay.

Chapter Fourteen

WE PLANNED TO MEET AT my apartment. I left work a little early, and picked up some things for a light dinner. I quickly made a tuna salad, sliced some apples, and toasted some bagels. They were on the table when she arrived.

"Hi", she said cheerfully, walking in. When she saw the food, she added, "Oh, I see you cooked."

"Now, now. Don't make fun of me."

"No. It looks perfect. And I'm hungry," she said with sincerity

When we sat down, I started, "Kathy, I thought about what you said yesterday. In fact, I haven't thought about anything else."

"Before you go on, let me say something. Just because I express some doubts to you, it doesn't mean I want this relationship to end. It's the most precious thing in the world to me. But you have to understand how difficult it is for me to go against values I've believed in all my life. I think in lots of ways you're a lot stronger than I am. You don't seem to need approval as much as I do."

"Approval from who?"

"From everyone. I'm the approval junkie. Haven't you figured that out yet?" I was shocked!

"No. I don't see you that way at all."

"I think you just see what you want to see."

"What I see is a confident, kind, caring and compassionate person," "And when I'm with you, I almost believe that."

"Kathy, everyone that knows you, adores you."

"But I only show them the parts of me I know they'll like. It's a game I've been playing my whole life. Until I met you." I wondered what parts she was talking about. Since she was so open with me, I just assumed she was that way with everyone.

"But we all do that. We all need approval."

"Not as much as I do." She paused. "Does it make you feel differently about me?"

"Not at all. At least you're aware that you do it. I suppose it's something you could change if you wanted to work on it. It makes me love you more." "How can you? I'm such a mess!"

"But the thing I like most about you is your openness and vulnerability. Besides that, you're the most beautiful, interesting and insightful person I've ever met in my life."

"So, you still want to be with me?" I never would have guessed that she felt insecure about my love for her.

"Of course. What is this, a test?" "Maybe."

"Did I pass?"

"You always pass. That's the problem." "Why is that a problem?" I asked.

"Because I don't think I'll ever find anyone else who loves me as unconditionally as you do."

"Well, I'm glad you finally realize that."

"Look, Susan. I didn't want to tell you this until I was sure of his plans, but I had a long talk with John last night and he wants to move Ann into the house."

"So what does that mean?" "It means I'm moving out." "And?" My heart was racing.

"And, how would you like to find a place with me? I want to live with you. I'm afraid if we don't try, I'll never have the chance again to have a relationship with someone I love as much as I love you."

"Oh my God," I screamed. And then, "Are you sure?"

"No, but what the heck. We'll never know unless we do it. Besides, you've been so grumpy lately, I have to do something to cheer you up," she said, smiling widely.

"Cheer me up! I'm delirious!"

"Anyway. I saw an ad in the paper for a place that sounds perfect. Want to see it? I made an appointment for 7:00."

The apartment complex was on a hill, but not overlooking the ocean. It overlooks the shopping center. "I don't mind," she said when she saw it. The inside was charming, with two big bedrooms, two bathrooms and a large living room and kitchen.

"What are we going to do with the extra bedroom?" I joked.

We put down a deposit and signed a lease for one year. We weren't moving in for two weeks, but the manager gave us a key, so that we could have some time to fix it up.

On the way back, Kathy excitedly talked about how she wanted to decorate it. "You know I'm going to be busy with Lynn's wedding, Kath, so I'm not going to have a lot of time to help."

"Yeah, I know. That means I can fix it up the way I like it."

"You can do anything you want to. The only thing I really care about is being there with you." I meant it. She was the only thing in the world I cared about.

As we said good night, she held me close. "Just think. In a few weeks, we won't have to say goodbye like this anymore."

"That will be heaven." I could hardly believe I could be this fortunate. I couldn't wait for my life with her to begin.

I set up an appointment with Mr. and Mrs. Parker. Patsy wanted to know why, since we had met for our regular therapy session less than a week ago.

"I'd rather discuss it with you in person."

When they were both seated in my office, I said, "We have a woman that's interested in meeting Teresa. She's been wanting to be a parent for many years, and would be thrilled to have an opportunity to adopt her." I tried to sound professional.

"Oh, my God. We thought she was too old to be adopted," Patsy said, genuinely surprised.

"There are many people out there that want to give children a good home, no matter how old they are." I couldn't hold in my disgust.

Ed was blunt. "So, do we sign something or what?"

"Yes. There are relinquishment forms to sign, but since Teresa is nearly fourteen, she would have the right to refuse. If Teresa agrees to the adoption, you'd have a year to change your minds. After that, all of your rights as parents would be terminated."

"We won't change our minds," Patsy said coldly.

"You're both sure this is what you want. You need to realize how final this is. There would be no contact at all with Teresa again." I still couldn't believe that Patsy would really choose to give up her child.

"Yes. Yes," Ed said impatiently. "Do we sign today?"

"You can. But part of the process would be for you and her brothers and sisters to say a final goodbye to Teresa."

"Why do we have to involve the other kids?" Patsy asked.

"Because Teresa has been a big part of their lives and they've been a big part of hers. You just can't make her disappear without an explanation. After the papers are signed, the other children won't be able to see Teresa again either. They all need some closure and a chance to say goodbye to each other."

"But they're glad she's gone. They never ask about her," Ed argued. I could barely keep from punching him!

"You do have a choice, but this is our agency's policy. If you don't agree to it, we may not be able to continue with the adoption." I tried to control my anger, but it was difficult.

They were silent. "I'm going to leave you alone to talk it over." I wanted to scream!

"No. We don't need to talk it over. We'll bring the kids in to say goodbye. We want this over as soon as possible." Patsy did the talking.

"I'll talk to Teresa tomorrow and then let you know when we want you to come in."

After they left, I called Mary to catch her up on what had been going on. I could hear Teresa in the background saying, "Let me talk to Susan."

"Hi Teresa."

"Susan, I got an A on my English test yesterday. I never got an A before." She wanted so much to succeed and have everyone be proud of her.

"I knew you were beautiful and smart the minute I saw you. It's a rare combination."

"And Mary and I went shopping yesterday and I got two pairs of new shoes."

"You really like it there, don't you Teresa?" I was so concerned about her reaction to moving again.

"Oh yes. Mary and Doug are the greatest." "Can you put Mary on the phone again?" "Sure. MARRRRY," she screamed.

"Hi Susan. Sorry about that." "Is she still there?"

"No, she went outside. What's up?"

"We found someone that may be interested in adopting her." There was dead silence on the other end.

"Are you still there, Mary?" "Yes, I'm here."

"I know this is a shock. Are you okay?"

"I guess we never thought you'd find anybody. We've gotten so attached to her."

"Can you and Doug come down here later. We need to talk about this."

Doug and Mary were hurting.

"Thanks for coming down. I can only imagine how hard this is for both of you. I know you really love Teresa."

"Yeah, we really do. We were talking about it the other night. We actually were thinking of approaching you about adopting her ourselves," Mary said.

"That doesn't surprise me at all. I think one of the hardest parts about being a foster parent is letting go. I don't know if I could do it." I wanted to let them know that their feelings were absolutely understandable. "How are you doing with this, Doug?"

"I love Teresa too, and I'll miss her, but I'm ok with it as long as she's going to be with someone who will treat her well."

"Actually, you're going to have a chance to meet the adoptive parent. In fact, you're going to be a big part of the whole process."

"Who will tell Teresa? Do you want us to do it?" Mary asked.

"We haven't worked out all the details yet, but I'll probably be the one to tell her. I'd want at least one of you there." They both looked so sad. I wanted to cheer them up. Just like I always wanted to cheer Kathy up when she looked sad. And mom. I was starting to understand that my discomfort of seeing people hurting and unhappy began with my mom. "You know, you guys, I'd really hate to lose you in the Foster Care Program, but if you'd like to become adoptive parents instead, I'll help you in any way I can."

Mary smiled. "What a sweet thing to say. I know you're really behind us, Susan. We appreciate your support so much. But we'll get over this. In fact, maybe it will help us do a better job with the next child. We'll be more realistic and know more about what to expect. I agree with Doug. As long as it's good for Teresa, I'm one hundred percent behind it -- even if it does hurt for now."

I explained the whole process to them and they both agreed to help as much as they could. When I finished, Mary said, "I'm just worried that Teresa will think that we're rejecting her too. After all, she's going to have to move again. I just want her to know that we really love her."

"I'm sure she knows that. It won't be the same as when she left her family. She's going to meet Betty first and get to know her. And, in the end, it will be her choice. We'll all be reassuring to her throughout the whole process." I had my doubts, but I wanted to believe that everything would work out well for Teresa.

"Ok. If you're going to handle it, I trust you." Mary answered. "We'll be in close contact throughout the whole thing. I promise."

Before they left, I hugged them both. I was beginning to feel like we were good friends. Isn't life funny? Teresa was a little girl that nobody wanted a few months ago. And now, look at all the people that really love her. Good for Teresa!

CHAPTER FIFTEEN

THE BIG DAY WAS FINALLY here. Lynn looked beautiful in a traditional white wedding gown. I was helping her with her hair, when Kathy popped in. Lynn invited her at the last minute as a gesture to me for helping her so much over the past few weeks. I had to point out to her though that if I had been with a man, he would have automatically been invited.

"Anything I can do to help?" Kathy had never seen me so dressed up, with makeup on. "Lynn, you look so beautiful. You too, Susan."

"Thank you. I'm glad you could come. Sorry it was so last minute," Lynn said apologetically.

I went over to her and whispered, "I'm so glad to see you." It was wonderful to have her there, but I couldn't help worrying that the wedding would remind her of what she had to give up to be with me. She pulled me over to a far corner.

"Susan, you look absolutely gorgeous. I can't take my eyes off of you." "Wait till you see what I look like when I get out of this thing," I teased. "Well, I'm sure I'll like that too."

"Come on, you guys," Lynn called out. "I'm the bride. I should get all the attention."

We all laughed. "Five minutes," someone yelled from outside the door. "I'd better get out of here and get a seat."

"Sit near the front, so I can see you," I whispered as I squeezed her hand. I turned to Lynn. "Well, this is it. Are you ready?"

"Let's hit it."

I went out first. Though the ceremony was in a small room and there were only about thirty guests, they made a space down the center for a short aisle. There was no music, but several people just started humming "Here Comes the Bride". Lynn appreciated that, and smiled widely as she marched in.

After the ceremony, there was a short reception, with champagne and a small wedding cake. Dennis looked very handsome in his tux and everyone commented what a good- looking couple they were.

I stood next to Kathy as they cut the cake and fed each other the first piece. Then they quickly hugged everyone goodbye before their flight to San Francisco.

"Just be happy, Lynn," I whispered as she put both of her arms around me. "I pray that everything works out well for you, Susan. You deserve it." She

looked at Kathy. "Take good care of her." Kathy smiled. "I will," she said. "I will."

My car was filled to the brim with everything I owned, which consisted of my clothes and a few personal things that I had collected over the years. Kathy and John had split up their furniture, so she had enough to give us a good start.

She had moved in the day before and was waiting outside as I drove up. "I got you a little housewarming gift," she said. "Why don't you come and look at it before we start taking your things up."

I followed her up the stairs. She had arranged her furniture in the living and dining rooms. It really looked terrific.

"Kathy, you did such a great job. It looks beautiful." I was truly impressed with her decorating skills. The living room looked very homey, with a couch and a loveseat placed by the fireplace. The TV was sitting separately, with another very comfortable little couch opposite it, so it looked like two little rooms instead of one big one. The way the furniture was arranged, it didn't look as though she was expecting much company. That was okay with me. I could be alone with her forever.

"Come on in here," she said, leading me to what was to be my bedroom. Inside was a complete bedroom set -- a bed, dresser, nightstand and lamp.

"Oh my God! When did you do this?" I was totally shocked and very touched that she would do this for me.

"It was just delivered this morning. Do you like it?" "Like it? I love it! But I can't let you pay for this."

"Well, you can pay for the dresser, but I want to pay for the bed. It's kind of a symbolic thank you and housewarming gift all in one."

"You're too much. What a thoughtful thing to do," I said hugging her. "Come on. Let's unpack your car and get you settled in."

After everything was in and put away, I tugged on her arm. "So, do you want to try out my new bed?" She laughed.

"Aren't you hungry? I'm starving."

As we ate dinner, I made a toast. "Here's to our new life together. May we always be as happy as we are right now."

She added, "Here's to you. You're not only my lover, you're the best friend I've ever had. No matter what happens, I hope that will never change." "It never will."

After we finished eating, she smiled. "So, let's go try out that new bed."

What surprised us both about living together were all the things that we didn't have in common. On weekends, I liked to sleep in; she liked to get up early. I liked to eat on the run; she liked to have sit-down dinners. I liked to stay up late; she liked to go to bed early. I liked sports; she liked needlepoint.

As we discovered new things about each other, we laughed about all the things we didn't know. We thought we had all areas covered. We would have long conversations about compromising. I easily agreed to go to bed early. We had wonderful talks lying in bed, holding each other. It was my favorite time of day.

In return, she agreed to pick up after herself. She had a habit of leaving clothes, dishes, papers, anything, all over the place. She actually got pretty good at it. I think it was mostly because she didn't like me nagging her.

We took turns cooking and doing the dishes. We both agreed that the meal was always better when it was her turn to cook. We divided up the chores; then traded every week so that everything would be absolutely fair.

I taught her how to play golf and poker; she taught me how to do needlepoint and knit.

We drove into work together every day and by now everyone knew we were living together. We agreed not to offer any explanations. We really didn't have to worry. No one ever asked us any questions about our private life.

Everyone at the office was anxious for Betty to meet Teresa, but we had to put things on hold. At the last minute, the Parker's decided they wanted an attorney to look over the relinquishment papers and they were taking their time getting them back to us.

That gave me time to put more energy into Joey. His mother had called me to arrange a visit with him. Children's Protective Services gave the okay as long as I was there to oversee the visit. His mom met me at the office, and I had Socorro bring Joey to a nearby park, since I didn't want Mona to know where he lived.

Mona was a short, stocky woman, with dark brown skin, black hair and brown eyes. She was clean and well groomed, dressed in a nice skirt and blouse. On the way to the park, she tried her best to convince me that she wasn't doing drugs. She talked about how much she loved Joey and how difficult it had been to raise him alone. She hardly knew his father. They had only gone out a few times before she got pregnant and she never told him that he had a son. She lived with her parents when Joey was a baby. Sometimes, she'd go on a drug binge and leave him for months at a time. After three or four times her parents threw her out. Then she and Joey had to make it on their own.

"That's a shame. No wonder Joey is so afraid to lose you." I knew what it was like to lose a father at a young age. It had to be worse to never have had one.

"I want him back, Miss Kramer. I've been going to counseling and I've been off drugs for three months now."

"It's not up to me, Mona. It's up to the courts. Have you been going to your drug program?"

"I don't need that. I told you, I quit."

I knew how difficult it was to quit on your own. I had worked in a drug treatment program in graduate school and the people who tried to quit on their own rarely succeeded. "But you've said that before and then started again."

"It's different this time. I know I have to quit for Joey."

"You have to quit for yourself first," I told her. "Or else it won't work."

"It will work, you'll see." I hoped for Joey's sake she was right. We drove the rest of the way in silence.

Joey was ecstatic when he saw his mother. "Mommy, mommy," he yelled as he ran to hug her.

"Joey, my boy, my boy," she said over and over. She took his hand and walked him far enough away so that I couldn't hear what they were saying.

"How are you, Socorro?" "Fine."

"Thanks for bringing him. How's he doing?"

"A little better I think. He doesn't swear as much."

We sat on the bench for about an hour and watched them laugh and play together. I found myself really rooting for her. She certainly did love him. And Joey was absolutely crazy about her.

No matter how much I enjoyed my job, I loved coming home at

night. Kathy and I would hug each other as soon as we got in and closed the door. I was incredibly happy.

One night as we sat on the patio, she asked, "Are you disappointed about anything living with me?"

"Only that you ask too many questions," I joked. "No, seriously."

"I love things just the way they are, but I know something's on your mind." I could always tell when she was worried about something.

"I'd just like to share us with more people." "So, you're getting sick of all this togetherness."

"No, that's not what I'm saying. It's just that sometimes I feel like we're hiding out."

"Really? I don't feel like that at all. I'm doing exactly what I want to." "But we can't live in a vacuum forever."

"So, do you want to do something about it?" I wasn't sure where this was going.

"Well, I was thinking it would be nice to have some other friends." "You mean gay friends?"

"Well, people we can feel comfortable around."

"I don't have any gay friends, do you?" She knew I was kidding. "I guess we could go to a gay bar. I'll bet we could find lots of gay women there."

"Come on, Susan. I'm serious."

"So am I. Do you want to go to a gay bar?" "I'd like to see what it's like."

"Okay. Let's go this weekend." "Are you sure?"

I laughed. "Yes, I'm sure. But don't ask me to dance."

CHAPTER SIXTEEN

SINCE WE MOVED IN TOGETHER, we had difficulty getting to work on time. We both loved cuddling together when we first woke up and it was hard to stop and get out of bed. This day was no exception. We were trying to sneak in the door without anyone seeing us.

"We're in here, ladies," Dave called out.

"Remember, don't look guilty," I whispered to Kathy. She smiled. The whole staff was sitting in the big meeting room.

"What's up?" I asked walking in.

"Great news," Mindy said. "Teresa's parents were here earlier and dropped off the signed relinquishment papers. Now we can move ahead."

"Move ahead with Teresa's final goodbye to her family or move with her meeting Betty?" I asked.

"I think meeting Betty should come first," Kathy said. "Then, if it doesn't work out, Teresa won't have to say goodbye to her family just yet. She'll have a little more time to adjust to the idea."

"That sounds great," I replied, trying to pretend we hadn't already discussed it at home. "I was thinking that Teresa would feel more comfortable if Doug and Mary could be there. What about a picnic in the park?"

"I don't know," Mindy said. "If Doug and Mary are there, Teresa won't interact with Betty as much."

"Why don't we invite all of the foster parents and all of the kids and have an agency party? That way there won't be as much pressure on Betty or Teresa," Kathy suggested.

"We could have a Bar-B-Q in the parking lot here. The whole staff can come," Dave added.

"So, is it settled?" Kathy asked.

"I guess," Mindy replied, disappointed that the meeting wasn't going to be more private.

As we walked out, Kathy winked at me. It worked out exactly as we had planned.

People started arriving at 4:30. Betty was the first one there. She waved when she saw me and came over to say hello. I introduced her to Kathy.

"You can't imagine how nervous I am," she admitted.

"You're going to love Teresa," Kathy said, trying to calm her down.

"I'm not worried about me liking Teresa. I'm worried about Teresa liking me."

I felt a little sorry for Betty. We really were putting her on the spot. Everyone on the staff knew the real reason for the Bar-B-Q and would be watching to see how things were going. But by her agreeing to meet Teresa in this way I liked her even more. Of course, what choice did she have?

As more people arrived, Kathy and I mingled, trying to make sure that everyone was properly introduced. We started some games for the kids, giving the foster parents a chance to catch up on each other's lives. Some of them hadn't seen each other since the training classes.

I didn't see Teresa arrive, so when I felt a tug on my arm and saw her standing beside me, I was surprised. "Hi Teresa. You look adorable."

"Do you like my new shoes?" she asked as she lifted her foot.

"Yeah, they look terrific on you." Doug and Mary had caught up with her and were standing by my side. "Hi, you guys. It's great to see you."

"Hey Mary and Doug, look who's here," Kathy called out as she pointed to some of the foster parents.

"Go on," I urged. "I'll keep an eye on Teresa."

Betty had been watching us from a short distance away. "Hey, Teresa. I'd like you to meet someone."

"Who?"

"Betty. She's a good friend of mine. Do you want to meet her?" "I guess." Her hesitation was obvious.

"Come on," I said, taking her hand. Betty smiled as we approached. "Betty, this is Teresa."

"Teresa, I've heard so much about you. I'm so glad to finally meet you." "Hi," Teresa said shyly.

"Do you like Bar-B-Q's?" Betty asked. "They're okay."

"Let's go over and get a hot dog. I like mine with mustard. What do you like on yours?"

To my surprise, Teresa followed her. "Ketchup," I heard her say as she walked off. I watched them, as Betty got two hot dogs and gave them to Teresa to put the condiments on top. Betty was doing most of the talking, but Teresa was smiling and seemed to enjoy the attention.

"Susan!" I turned around to see Joey waving and running toward me. "Hey, Joey. How's my guy?" I stooped down to hug him.

"I told you my mom was going to get me back." I hadn't seen him since we met in the park.

"Yes, you did. I liked your mom a lot, Joey. And I can see that she's mad about you." He just beamed and ran off to get some food.

"Who is that adorable little boy?" Mary asked. "Oh, that's Joey. He's a real character."

"How do you think it's going, Susan?" I couldn't blame Mary for being anxious.

We both looked in Betty's direction. She was showing Teresa some pictures.

"Let's keep our fingers crossed," I answered hopefully. Then I joined Kathy, who was having a great time with the kids. They were playing "Hot Potato" and laughing with glee every time someone else was eliminated.

"Come and play," one of the kids shouted out. "In a minute, you guys."

I walked back to where Teresa and Betty were sitting. "Look, Susan," Teresa said holding a picture out so that I could see it. "This is Betty's dog. His name is Buddy. And this is her house. She lives near the beach and asked me if I'd like to go swimming sometime."

"Would you like to go to Betty's house, Teresa? I can arrange it." "Oh yes. I'd like to."

"Let's see if it's okay with Mary. Why don't you run over and ask her." After she left, I turned to Betty. "It's going well, I assume."

"I'm already crazy about her. She's such a sweet child. She seems so much younger than thirteen."

"Yes, I know. She's doing a lot better though since she's been with Doug and Mary. We're hoping that as she gets the attention she needs, she'll catch up to kids her age pretty quickly. She's got a fairly high IQ."

Teresa came running back. "It's okay," she yelled excitedly. "Great," Betty said. "I'll arrange it with Susan and Mary."

Everyone seemed to have a good time, except Mindy. She really got left out of the loop. I went over to her after everyone had left. "It really went well, didn't it?" I tried to make her feel important about her contribution.

"Yeah, Susan. I'm really happy for them both."

"Thanks for all your help, Mindy. I think we work well together."

"Thanks."

On the way home, Kathy touched my arm softly. "You did a great job, Susan. I'm really proud of you." I always felt especially good when she told me she liked the work I was doing with people. It meant a lot coming from someone who was so good at it herself.

"I couldn't have done it without you."

"Yes, you could. And you did. I just gave a little moral support every once in a while."

"You were wonderful. You are wonderful." I felt so much love for her. "Only with you, honey. Only with you."

I waited a few days before driving out to see Teresa. She came out the front door when she saw my car. She smiled widely and came running over to me. I gave her a big hug. She took my hand and led me into the house.

"Mary," she called. "Susan's here."

"Hi, Susan. I'm making lunch. Are you hungry?" "I could eat something."

"Mary's a real good cook, Susan. And she's teaching me. I can bake a cake and make spaghetti."

"That's wonderful, kiddo." I decided to talk to Teresa about the adoption in front of Mary. I knew that she would make things easier for Teresa, and that she would be very supportive towards me. Heaven knows, I needed all the support I could get.

When we sat down, I said, "Hey, Teresa. Remember when you were in my office?" I wanted her to make the connection with what our purpose is at the agency.

"Yeah, I remember. That was the first day I met you."

"Well, not only do we find foster homes for kids, but some of the people who work there look for people who want to adopt children permanently. Do you know what it means to be adopted?"

"Yes. Some kids are orphans -- they don't have any parents. So then they can be adopted by other parents."

"That's right. Well, you remember Betty, the woman you met at the picnic, don't you?"

"Of course. I'm going to go to her house soon so that I can go to the beach." "Betty is looking for a girl to adopt. A girl like you."

"But Susan, I already have parents."

"Yes, I know. But, sometimes, a child has parents that they can't live with. So, if that happens, then we can try to find other parents for them." This was really hard for me and I didn't think I was doing a very good job. But I knew it was much harder for Teresa.

"Oh." She looked confused and turned to Mary.

"So, when you left home, just in case you couldn't go back, I told the adoption workers to find a parent for you. So they did. They found Betty. And if you spend some time with her and like her, then Betty wants to adopt you. She already likes you so much." I knew it was way too complicated for her to understand fully at this point so I tried to simplify it as much as possible.

"Oh Susan, that's wonderful news," Mary chimed in. "Isn't that terrific, sweetie," she said, turning to Teresa.

"But does that mean I'd have to leave here?" She had a look of panic on her face.

"Well, yes. But we'll still be able to see you. Doug and I love you, honey. We want you to be happy. This is such a wonderful chance for you."

"But I'm happy here with you," she said, close to tears.

"Well, you don't have to decide now. Why don't you get to know Betty? Then you can decide if you want to live with her or not." Mary said it as casually as she could.

"Mary's right, Teresa. I won't make you go and live with someone else unless you really want to. And until you're ready, you can stay here."

"Will I still get to see my parents?" she asked.

"You know, you're going to be so busy, you probably won't even have time to think about seeing them." I didn't really expect her to believe this. I didn't even believe it.

"Yes I will."

"Well, let's not worry about that right now. We just need to decide if you'd like to spend some time with Betty. She really wants to get to know you." I didn't want her to have to deal with the permanent loss of her parents now. It was just too much to process all at once.

"I guess so," she said without enthusiasm.

"You don't seem very happy about this, Teresa."

"I don't want to leave Mary." I certainly understood how she felt and sympathized greatly.

"Do you wonder why you just can't stay here? Do you wonder why Doug and Mary can't adopt you?"

She didn't answer. I looked helplessly at Mary. "I know this is really hard for you, honey. Doug and I are foster parents. That means we keep kids temporarily while the agency finds another home. Remember, we explained it to you when you first came."

"I remember," Teresa said sadly.

"But I promise you won't have to go and live with Betty unless you really want to," I reassured her.

"Okay. I'll go to her house. But that doesn't mean I want her to adopt me." "Oh, Betty will be so happy. You know I would never do anything that

would be bad for you, don't you? And I will never force you to do anything you didn't want to do. You believe me, don't you?"

"Yes. I believe you."

"It will be okay, I promise." I was trying hard to be positive, but the truth was that I hated moving Teresa again.

When Teresa left, Mary asked, "Do you think she'll be okay, Susan?"

"I hope so. I'm really not planning on pressing her to make a quick decision. She can take all the time she needs. You were really wonderful with her. I can understand why she wouldn't want to leave." I gave her a warm hug goodbye.

As I walked to my car, I felt sad for both of them. And for the first time since I started, I really hated this job!

CHAPTER SEVENTEEN

NEITHER ONE OF US HAD ever been to a gay bar, but I knew where they were. The nicest looking one from the outside was close to where we worked. It flashed through my mind that we might see someone we knew, but I decided not to worry about it.

When we got there, we sat in the car for a while, trying to get up the nerve to go in. Finally, I asked, "Are you ready?"

"I don't know why I'm so nervous about this."

"I'm nervous too. It's a big step." I wasn't sure what I was more nervous about, the bar or Kathy's reaction to it. Things had been going so well. I didn't want her to start having doubts again.

There was a live female band on stage. It sounded more like loud noise than music. A long bar took up the front of the large room. There were about twenty small tables spread out in front of the stage. "Let's sit at the bar," I said.

It was dark and smoky. It took a few minutes for our eyes to adjust. Several of the tables were filled with women and there were many "couples" on the dance floor. An attractive female bartender came over.

"What can I get for you ladies?"

I ordered a coke. Kathy ordered white wine.

"I haven't seen you in here before. Are you new to the area?"

"Yes. We just moved in a couple of months ago." Kathy tried to be friendly. "Well, enjoy yourselves. No one will bother you here."

We sipped our drinks. "Let's go to a table." I took her hand and led her to one at the side. She pulled her hand away as we sat down. "It's okay to hold my hand here. Remember?"

"It just feels so weird. I'm not comfortable at all." It felt strange to me too. I never held hands with a woman in public before.

"Me either. But let's stay for a while. Maybe it will get better."

A couple at the next table smiled. I smiled back. "Why don't you come over and join us?" one of them asked.

Kathy was frozen. "Sure," I answered. "Let's go honey." I practically dragged her over.

"I'm Susan. This is my partner, Kathy." "This is Grace and I'm Bonnie."

We shook hands and sat down. They looked about fifty, with short, gray hair, and wrinkled skin. They were dressed similarly in blue jeans and long-sleeved western shirts. They both looked tired. And, to me, they looked depressed.

"So, are you guys new in the area?" It must be the standard opening question, I thought.

"We moved here a few months ago."

"We love it here in Long Beach. We've been together for sixteen years. I met Grace right here in this bar. We come about two times a week."

"Wow." Kathy tugged at my arm. "Let's dance, Susan." We had already talked about not dancing so I was really taken aback.

"Excuse us," I said and followed her to the dance floor. "Is something wrong?"

"Look, I made a big mistake. I want to leave." I was disappointed that she didn't want to give it more of a chance.

"As long as we're here, let's just have one dance. I can manage a slow one." She hesitated. "Come on," I said holding out my arms.

She smiled and put her arms around me. We just stood there. Finally, I said, "Someone's got to lead."

She hardly said a word all the way home.

"I know you're upset, Kath. Was it really that bad?"

"It was horrible. That dingy little bar with those sad-looking people. I never want to go there again." I was surprised at the depth of her revulsion.

"Well, we don't have to."

"I'm going to sleep in my own room tonight, Susan. I just need a little space."

"You're acting like it's my fault."

"It's not your fault. But I don't think you ever look beyond us. We still have to interact with other people. And when I see how society treats people like us, it scares me. It's not accepted. So we have to sneak around and hide in sleazy little bars. I don't want any part of it. I don't want to end up like those women we saw in there."

I wanted to make her feel better, but I didn't know how. So, I didn't say anything.

"I'll see you in the morning." She came over and gave me a peck on the cheek. Then she went to her room and closed the door.

I couldn't sleep. I wanted to go to her, but I was afraid that she would reject me and then I'd feel worse. All I could do was hope that she would feel better about things in the morning.

I must have dozed off. I felt her put her arm around me and press her body against my backside. "Are you awake?" Thank God, I thought. I was so relieved that she was here.

"Now I am," I mumbled. "I'm so sorry if I hurt you."

"I know. We can work it out. I don't want to lose you."

"I love you, Susan. But sometimes, it's just such a struggle for me. I just feel so guilty."

"Do you really think God would punish you for loving me? How can something so beautiful be wrong?"

"I don't have the answers. I just have the questions." She paused. "I'm exhausted. I can't sleep without you."

I turned over on my back and she put her head on my chest. I wrapped by arms around her and held her close. She fell asleep in my arms.

CHAPTER EIGHTEEN

OVER THE NEXT FEW MONTHS, Teresa spent every weekend with Betty. When she came back to Doug and Mary's house, she would talk excitedly about what they did together. She loved Betty's dog, Buddy, and loved being so close to the beach. She really liked Betty too. What kid wouldn't? Every weekend she planned something special for Teresa. Teresa loved to go shopping and Betty loved helping her pick out new clothes. She bought her one or two new outfits every week. Mary and I would tease Teresa that we wished Betty would adopt us too.

I saw her regularly to monitor her progress. Teresa had mixed feelings. "She's so nice to me, Susan. But I feel bad about leaving Mary and Doug."

I kept reassuring her that Doug and Mary wanted her to be happy. "We all do." I also explained to her that after she moved in with Betty, I would still come to see her. "And Betty told me that you could talk to Mary or Doug any time you wanted to."

Betty didn't pressure her, but she confided in me that it was getting more and more difficult for her to take her back. "I'm trying so hard to be patient. But I've waited so long for a child, that these last few weeks have been really tough." I empathized. I remember how hard it was to leave Kathy before we moved in together.

I felt very positive about Betty. So did Doug and Mary. They knew it was the best possible match for Teresa. We were just waiting for Teresa to make up her mind. When she finally did, the rest of the process moved very quickly. I happened to be there when Betty brought

Teresa home one afternoon. She sat between Doug and Mary and held their hands. Then she said, "Are you sure it would be okay with you if I moved in with Betty?" Doug squeezed her hand. "We just want you to be happy, sweetheart," he answered. "Okay, then I will." It was just that simple. The day before she moved, Doug and Mary gave her a party and invited all of her friends from school. Teresa introduced Betty as her new mom. Betty was very touched. I finally felt more confident that we were doing the best thing for Teresa.

About three weeks after she moved and we were sure that Teresa was comfortable, we arranged for her farewell to her family. Patsy, Ed and their five children were waiting in our conference room when I brought Teresa in. Patsy had made an album to give to her. This act of kindness really surprised me. It contained pictures of all of her brothers and sisters as well as pictures of Teresa at different ages of her young life. She included a picture of herself. Pictures of Ed were noticeably missing. After looking through it with Teresa, Patsy began her final goodbye.

"Teresa, we're so happy for you that you found a new home and will have all of the things that we couldn't give you. We want you to enjoy your new life. We'll think of you often. We hope you understand why we made this decision." I stood next to Teresa and kept my hand on her shoulder. I felt terrible that we were making her do this. I understood the concept, but I thought the actual process of giving the family closure was very hard on everyone concerned, especially Teresa.

"Is there anything you want to say Teresa?" I knew that Mary had helped her rehearse this day many, many times.

"Thank you for everything you've done for me. I'll always remember each one of you. You'll always be in my heart." By the time she got to the end, the tears were flowing down her cheeks. She said it perfectly. I was so proud of her for doing it. It was almost as if she grew up in that one moment.

One at a time, her sisters and brothers came over and hugged her.

She held each one and tried to smile. "I love you," she almost shouted as they walked out of the room. Then Ed walked over and gave her an awkward hug. "Goodbye, Teresa," he muttered, and looked angrily in my direction as he left the room. By then I was too choked up to even care.

Patsy looked at Teresa for a long time before she walked over to her. She took her daughter's tear-stained face in both of her hands. "I know I'm doing the right thing. I hope someday you'll understand and forgive me."

"Mama, don't leave," Teresa cried as Patsy turned and walked out of the room.

I put my arms around her and led her to the couch. I held her for a long time as she cried. Then Betty appeared at the door and I motioned for her to come in. She put her hand on Teresa's shoulder. "It's okay, honey. It's okay." What an ordeal! I kind of wished that Betty would comfort me too.

I called Mary to let her know it was over. "You know, I actually think she had a harder time saying goodbye to you and Doug."

"We talked to Betty. She wants us to come down later to see her."

"I think that's a good idea. As she gets more adjusted though, you know you'll have to taper off the visits." "Yeah, we know."

"Thanks for being so terrific to her."

"It was easy. She's a great kid. We feel lucky to have had her for the time that we did. Thanks for all your help."

"Do you want a break or are you ready for a new foster child right away." "The sooner the better."

I felt really sad too. Now that Teresa was transferred to the adoption program, Mindy would be doing the home visits. When Kathy first told me, I argued, but she got me to understand that it was best for Teresa. "She needs to move on with her new life. You'll just remind her of the old one."

I felt selfish. It was like losing my first-born! "Do we have to do it now? My God, she's already said goodbye to so many people." And so have I!

"No, but soon. Mindy will be going on home visits with you for now. We want you to stay in the background so that Teresa can attach to her. Then you'll slowly drop out of the picture."

She could tell that I was upset. "Susan, I know it's hard but you're going to have to learn to let go or you won't survive here."

"I know that you're right. But give me a break. This is my first time." I really could understand what Doug and Mary must be going through. Only it was much worse for them. How I admired the way they handled it.

She smiled. "Well, I'm going home. Are you coming?"

"You said the magic words." I was so grateful for my life with her.

CHAPTER NINETEEN

WE JUST FINISHED LUNCH AND were headed out the door when the phone rang.

"Let's just go," Kathy said. We were going to a movie and running late. "It might be Lynn. I haven't heard from her in a while."

"Susan, this is Dave." I knew right away from the tone of his voice that something was wrong.

"What is it, Dave?" Kathy came back into the room and looked at me with concern.

"It's about Mona. She OD'd sometime during the night. She's dead."

"Oh my God, Joey." He would be absolutely devastated. What a disaster for him!

"We think you should be the one to tell him. He trusts you more than anyone. We don't really know any of the details yet. A neighbor found her and called the police."

"What's going to happen to Joey?" Kathy grabbed my hand. I was shaking. "I think he'll be able to stay where he is for the time being. Maybe a relative will show up and be able to take him."

"Do you think I should go out there today?" "Yes."

"Well, I'll leave now." "Thanks, Susan."

When I hung up, Kathy hugged me. "Oh God, Kath, that poor little boy. How do I tell him his mother is dead?" She held me as I cried.

"Why don't I go with you? I think I can help."

"I don't know who's going to need more help, me or Joey," I said through my tears.

126

I called Socorro to let her know what had happened. "Oh no, all he talks about since that day in the park is going back to live with his mother."

"Can you make sure he doesn't wander off? I'll be there within the hour." I could tell she was holding back tears. "Okay. I'll make sure he's here."

"I don't think I can do this, Kathy. He's going to be heartbroken." I started to cry again.

"Susan, you'll have to be strong for Joey."

"I know." I paused. "I was thinking how I would feel if I ever lost you." "This is hardly the time to think about that. Besides, you're not going to lose me."

"You can't say that for sure. Mona probably said that to Joey hundreds of times."

"Look, this isn't helping Joey. You have to think about him now." "You're right." I paused. "Just stay by me in case I break down." "I will. We'll get through it." She was always so supportive.

Joey ran up to the car as we pulled in the driveway. He looked so happy. "Hey, Joey," I said, hugging him. "This is Kathy. She works with me. Remember, you met her at the Bar-B-Q a few months ago."

"Oh yea. Hi, Kathy. Have you seen my mom, Susan? She hasn't called me in a few days."

"Well, that's what we came to talk to you about. Let's go inside."

"Hi Socorro," I said walking in. "Is it okay if we visit with Joey for a while?"

She led us into the den. Joey just stood there, waiting.

"Come over here, Joe." I wanted him close so I could hold him. "Just tell me, Susan." Suddenly he seemed so grown up.

"Joey, your mother died this morning."

He just stood there staring at me. He didn't move. He didn't even blink.

I went over to him and put my hand on his shoulder. "Did you hear me, Joey?"

He jerked away and ran out of the room. Socorro grabbed him, but Kathy yelled, "Let him go, Socorro." He ran up to his room and slammed the door.

We decided to leave him alone for a while, but we heard loud bangs, like he was throwing things against the wall and the door. "We need to help him. We'd better go up," Kathy said in an urgent tone of voice.

Socorro led the way. "Let me go in first." Kathy took charge. "Joey, it's Kathy and Susan."

"Go away," he shouted.

"No. We're coming in." I was so grateful Kathy was there. I was a wreck!

When we opened the door, he tried to lunge at it from the other side, but wasn't strong enough to keep us out. I grabbed him around the waist. He tried to punch me, but Kathy stopped him by holding his arms. "Joey," she said softly. "I'm so sorry about your mother. I know how much you loved her."

He started to cry, and as he did, his body went limp. Kathy let go of his arms and he wrapped them around my neck, burying his face in my shoulder. "I'm here, Joey. I'll be here for you." I just held him as he sobbed, stroking his back, his hair, his head. Then I picked him up and put him on his bed. "Poor little guy, he's exhausted," Kathy said softly.

Socorro stood at the doorway. "Will he be okay?"

"He may be a handful for a while. Do you think you can handle it?" Kathy asked.

She nodded yes and they stepped out in the hallway.

I just rubbed his back softly as he sobbed. Finally, he turned around and looked at me. "Why did she die?" he cried. "She promised me she would get me back. Why did she lie to me?"

"She didn't lie to you, Joey. But when she used drugs she was a different person. She loved you so much. You were the most important thing in the world to her."

"That's not true. Drugs were more important."

"I don't think so, Joey. She just couldn't control the drugs. That's what addiction means. She didn't understand that. She thought she could handle it by herself. But she needed help."

"I told her I'd help her."

"I know. But she needed professional help too."

He was quiet for several minutes. Then he asked, "What's going to happen to me?"

"You can stay here for now. And I'll come to see you often. You don't have to worry about anything. I promise you'll be safe."

He turned over again. I rubbed his back until he fell asleep.

On the way home, Kathy told me that she talked to Socorro about how to help Joey through this. I didn't say anything. I just prayed he'd be okay.

When we got home I went to my room. I had to lie down. Kathy followed and got into bed next to me. She didn't say anything. She just held me.

I could feel the tears welling up deep inside me. I couldn't stop it. And, in an instant, I was sobbing. Kathy held me tighter. "Just let it go, honey. I'm here. I'll help you. Just let it go."

I knew the tears weren't for Joey anymore, but somehow watching him feel his pain allowed me to get in touch with my own. For the first time, I cried for my mom and my sister. Kathy knew it too.

"Kathy, they're gone. They're really gone. Mom. Annie. Oh my God. No.

No." I could hardly breathe. My head was throbbing. But I couldn't stop. I had held it in so long. The loss I felt was almost unbearable. Kathy talked to me softly, but I couldn't hear what she said. I felt her arms around me. It was the only thing that made it real.

"I loved them so much. It's just so hard to accept," I said when I was finally able to talk. And then I started crying all over again. And, still, she held me. She held me until I cried myself to sleep.

When I woke up the next morning I was still in her arms. "Good morning, sweetheart," she said lovingly.

I felt weak and embarrassed. "Kathy, I'm so sorry about last night..."

"Don't ever apologize for showing your feelings to me, Susan. I want to be there for you. I love it when you open up to me." She held me tighter. "Tell me about your mom."

I took a deep breath. It was still hard for me to talk about her. "I remember when I was in the seventh grade, I had to write a paper describing my favorite person. At the risk of certain teasing from my classmates, I wrote my paper about my mom. I don't remember all the details, but I talked about her kindness, gentleness, selflessness, and her ability to make all three of us feel like the most special children in the world---and the most loved. My mom saved that paper for years. She was very proud of it. I wish you could have known her. In those early years, before my dad died, she was a wonderful mother -- the best.

"And then when he died, her life became such a struggle. She did her best and never complained. And for a long time, she put her children first. She helped my brother through college and, when she had the money, she would buy clothes for Annie and me before she'd spend any money on herself.

"Every fall she would take us shopping. She knew it was an ordeal for us -- we both hated to try on clothes in the small dressing rooms. So after a morning of shopping, she would take us to lunch and a movie. And the day would become a wonderful outing. I cherish those times I spent with her. Mom and Annie were my best friends. And then, when she got sick, it all ended."

I started crying all over again. "It's okay, honey. I'm here. I'm here."

Over the next few weeks, I talked to Kathy a lot about my mom and sister. I confessed how guilty I felt about how I treated Annie when we were younger. "Annie was the nicest, most thoughtful, considerate person in the world. I know my mom didn't mean to hurt me, but when she was angry with me, she'd say, 'Why can't you be good like your sister?'

I grew to resent Annie and when I made a new friend, I wanted to keep her for myself. I didn't want to share her with Annie. Annie was really hurt. I didn't know it at the time, but I think I was always afraid that my friend would like Annie better.

Thank god, when we grew up, she forgave me for all of that. About six months before the accident, I told Annie that I thought I was gay. She was so loving and supportive. I was always so grateful I had her in my corner."

"She sounds like a wonderful person. I hope my sister is that understanding."

"So do I, my love. So do I."

"Susan, you're my best friend. I want so much to fill that void for you."

"Oh Kath, you've been so important to me. You're the best friend I could have ever hoped for. I feel so lucky to have you. Don't ever doubt that."

She smiled. Then we made love. All was right with my world.

CHAPTER TWENTY

"DO YOU THINK YOU CAN get along without me for four or five days? Jenny just called and wants me to help her with the wedding. It's only six months away."

"Do you want to go?"

"Not really, but I'd feel selfish if I said no. After all, I am her only sister." "Of course. When are you going?"

"I was thinking about next week."

"Wow, so soon?" I was missing her already. "Well, I think it's just better to get it over with."

"Whatever you say. You know, you really didn't need my permission, but I appreciate that you asked. Thank you."

She smiled. "I guess we're really a couple, huh." "Yeah. I'll try to stay out of trouble while you're gone." "You'd better," she said, giving me a pat on my rear.

The night before she left, she was in a somber mood. "You know, I really don't want to go."

"The time will go fast. You'll be so busy. I've made some plans with Lynn and I plan to see Joey a few times. It will be okay." I was trying to convince myself as much as I was trying to convince her.

"I just have a bad feeling about it. Maybe it's nothing. Are you sure you're all right with it? I just don't want to leave you now."

"I know. You've helped me so much these past few weeks. I feel so close to you. But you'll be home before you know it." I paused and smiled. "Come here. Let me try to make it better."

She came over and sat on my lap. I squeezed her against me. "Mmm, it's better already," she whispered. Then she slid down between my legs and kissed my thighs. She reached up and tugged at my gym shorts. I lifted my body so she could slide them off. It always amazed me how excited I got from her touch. She kissed my groin through my panties. Then she pulled the silky material to one side and ran her tongue down my bare skin. I closed my eyes and put my legs on her shoulders as she kissed and licked me until my body shook out of control. "That was wonderful," I whispered. "That's so you don't forget me."

I pulled her up off the floor so that her face was level with mine. "Well, I guess I'll have to do something to make sure you don't forget me."

"And what would that be?"

"Why don't you just close your eyes and find out."

We were late getting to the airport, so I just dropped her off at the curb. I gave her a quick hug. "I'm really going to miss you," I said, holding back tears. I didn't want her to go. I couldn't help thinking about the last time I said goodbye to mom and Annie. I couldn't bear losing Kathy now.

"Me too. I'll call you tonight."

I watched her walk into the terminal. She turned around and waved. I blew her a kiss and tried to reassure myself that it couldn't happen a second time. I found myself praying for the first time in years -- "Please God, keep Kathy safe."

The apartment was so empty without her. I had to get out and do something. I decided to visit Joey. He was still having such a hard time accepting his mother's death and Socorro was having a very difficult time handling his anger. She told me we'd have to find another home for him unless something was done. He was having temper tantrums that were scary to her children, Javier and Maria. The doctor put him on an anti-depressant medication. At the time I was against it, but I had to admit that he was calmer since he started taking it.

He was watching television when I arrived. He looked at me, but didn't smile. "Hi Joey. Want to go out for a hamburger?"

"I'm not very hungry."

"You don't want a hamburger? That's a first," I teased. "Well, then let's just go for a ride."

He got up and walked to the door, then waited as I went to find Socorro. By the time I got back, he was sitting in my car. He didn't say anything for several minutes.

"I know that it's hard, Joey. I know you miss your mom and feel very alone. But trust me. You won't always be alone."

"Why should I trust you? You're just like my mother. Making promises you can't keep. She'd tell me, 'You'll see. I'm going to get better and get you back!' She lied to me. And you're lying too."

"I know you think that now. But in time, I hope you'll understand things differently."

"What do you mean?"

"I mean that the pain you feel now will heal and you'll be able to go on with your life."

"Come on. Don't give me that shit."

"Joey, I know that you're angry. I understand. Really I do." I wanted to tell him about my mom and Annie, but not now. It just wasn't the right time.

He didn't answer. Even though he wasn't hungry, I bought him a hamburger. "Save it for later." When I dropped him off, I said, "There are a lot of people who still care about you, including me." He got out of the car without saying goodbye.

I drove around for a while, remembering how angry I was at my mother for all those years. And I remembered the sense of relief that I felt when I could finally let it all go and forgive her. I wanted Joey to feel that sense of relief, but I knew it would take time. The only thing I could do was be there for him, hope he'd learn to trust me again, and begin to open up.

"Hi sweetheart," I said when I heard her voice. I was so relieved. "How was your trip?"

"It was fine, but I miss you."

"I know. I miss you too. The apartment is so empty. I think I'll sleep in your bed tonight. It will make me feel closer to you."

She laughed. "Jenny asked about you. I really think I'm going to tell her about us, Susan. I just hate lying to her. She's going to find out eventually. The longer I wait, the harder it will be."

"I wish I could be there to help." I was worried. After meeting Jenny and knowing how negative she was about being gay, I couldn't see how talking to her could be a positive experience for Kathy.

"It helps just knowing you're there waiting for me to come home." "You can think about the welcome I'll give you when you get here." "What have you been doing?"

"I went to see Joey. He's still so upset. He's angry at everyone, even me." "It takes time to get over a shock like that."

"I know. It just hurts to see him so unhappy. Almost as much as I hate to see you unhappy."

"I hope you don't think I'm unhappy with you. I love you, Susan."

"I know you do. And I love you. Hurry home. And call me if you need some moral support." I knew Kathy would need more than moral support if her sister didn't approve of her new lifestyle. After all, she's the approval junkie.

"I will. See you soon, my love." "Goodnight, Kath."

I did some chores around the house, but I still felt restless. Lynn and Dennis were busy with other friends and there wasn't anyone else I could call. We really had become very isolated in our own little world. I didn't realize how much until she was gone.

I got in my car and started driving. I pretended I was just going for a ride, but I knew where I would end up. I felt drawn to it. I just wanted to be around other lesbians. The bar was more crowded than it was the night Kathy and I were there. I stood at the door for a moment, taking everything in, and then decided to sit on one of the empty stools at the bar. I ordered a drink and turned around so that I could watch the women who were crowded on the dance floor. Some of them looked my age and several were very attractive. I hardly noticed the young woman sitting on the stool next to me.

"Are you new to the area? I haven't seen you in here before."

I looked at her and smiled. "That seems to be a popular opening line." "Excuse me?"

"I'm sorry. I've only been here once before and talked to two people. Both of them approached me with that same question. It just struck me funny. I didn't mean to be rude."

"Maybe I'll have to be more original from now on. Are you here alone?" "I'm here alone, but I'm not unattached," I said awkwardly. "My partner is

out of town. I'm just looking for some friendly conversation."

"It never fails. All the beautiful women are always taken. My name is Lena."

"I'm Susan."

"Hi Susan. It's nice to meet you." I awkwardly shook her hand. "You seem uncomfortable, are you?"

"A little."

"You haven't been out for long, have you?" "It depends on what you mean by out."

She hesitated. "I guess I mean letting people know that you're gay. You are gay, aren't you?"

"Yes. But when you put it like that, you can definitely say I'm still in the closet. Are you out?" I asked.

"Mostly. But I don't really talk about it much. And I'm not out at work." "Why not?"

"I'm a teacher. Need I say more."

"So. You're out to your family and friends?"

"Most of my friends now are gay. I rarely see the friends I grew up with. They really don't understand and I sense they're uncomfortable around me. I don't get invited to their family functions anymore. They won't say it, but I think I'm an embarrassment to them."

"That must hurt." I really felt sorry for her.

"It did at first, but I'm over it now. I can't really blame them. They've been taught all of their lives that being gay isn't normal. Why would that change all of a sudden?"

Her response irritated me. "It should change because they care about you. You should show them that you're the same person you've always been and that loving a woman can be just as beautiful as loving a man." I was thinking about Kathy when I said it. I didn't want her to go through the same kind of rejection that Lena was talking about.

"Whoa, hold on there."

"I'm sorry. I just get so upset when I hear stuff like that."

She didn't respond and turned away. I felt badly that I had upset her but after a minute, she turned back to me.

"So, Susan in the closet, would you like to dance?"

I hesitated. "No. If I danced with you, I'd feel like I was cheating. When Kathy comes back, I don't want to tell her any lies."

"Then, why are you here?"

"I told you. I'm just looking for some friendly conversation." "Well, I hope you find it. See you around." And with that, she left.

I ordered another drink and took it to an empty table. Maybe I should have danced with her, I thought. No. If I did, it would have led her on and I didn't want to do that. So, for the next half hour I sat alone and watched the women talk and dance together. Many of them appeared to be having a great time. I felt jealous of the ease and comfort they seemed to feel in public. I wondered if Kathy and I could ever be that comfortable. The way things were now, it was hard to imagine that ever happening.

"I see you're still here," Lena said, as she came up behind me holding a drink. "I thought you left."

"No. I just moved. Want to sit down?" She hesitated.

"Please. You're the first lesbian I've really talked to. I'm truly interested in what it's been like for you."

"But Kathy's a lesbian."

"Well, I don't think she'd describe herself that way. I'm her first female lover. And she's struggling a lot with the relationship. She is not out to her family and doesn't think they'll accept it."

"And you?"

"I'm not struggling with loving her, but it's difficult to feel comfortable because I worry that she'll leave me."

"I can't imagine anyone wanting to leave you."

"Thanks. I need all the reassurance I can get! So, have you decided to sit down and join me?"

"I'd like to. You seem like a really nice person, but I have other things on my mind, if you know what I mean, and you're not available!" she said with a wink.

"Oh." I blushed. "Can I just ask you one more thing?" "What's that?"

"You said before you're out to your family. How did they handle it?"

"My sister was great. She wants me to do whatever makes me happy. My mom does too. But my dad has a hard time with it. He barely talks to me when I go back home to see them. I've never introduced them to any of my gay friends. I'm not sure how my father would react and I wouldn't want to put anyone through a possible rejection."

"Well, at least you have the support of your mom and sister."

"Yeah, it means a lot to me. But I think it's more tolerance than support." Again, I felt very sad for her.

"Well, good luck with your search," I kidded. "I really need to get going."

She smiled and took my hand again. Only this time she didn't shake it. She held it, then put it to her lips and kissed it. "Goodnight Susan in the closet. I hope to meet you again someday when you're not so tied up."

"That won't happen, Lena. There'll never be anyone else for me."

As I walked to my car, all I could think about was Kathy. And I prayed that coming out to her sister would go well. God help her -- and me -- if it didn't.

CHAPTER TWENTY-ONE

DAVE CALLED ME INTO HIS office when I walked into work the next morning. "We've got a problem, Susan. Socorro called. She wants us to find another place for Joey. She just can't handle him anymore. He punched Javier in the mouth last night and they had to take him to the ER. They dropped Joey off here this morning. He's in the playroom. Do you think Doug and Mary can handle him?"

"Yes, I think so. Doug's much more available than Manuel was and he can spend a lot of time with Joey. He can really use a good father figure about now."

"Why don't you call them? I'll go down and check on Joey."

When Mary answered the phone, I explained what had happened to Mona and why Socorro couldn't keep Joey. "I don't want to pressure you but if we can't place him with you he'll have to go back to a group home"

"We were just talking last night about how lonely we've felt since Teresa left. We were hoping you'd call soon with a new child. Let me talk to Doug and call you right back."

I walked down to the playroom. Dave was on the floor playing a game with Joey. He looked up when I walked in. "Hi Susan. I guess I really screwed up. I'm sorry."

After Dave left, I asked, "What happened?"

"I got mad because Javier took my watch. My mother gave it to me for my birthday."

"I know that watch was important to you but there must be more to it than that."

He told me that he had traded his watch for a baseball glove. Then he had second thoughts about it and wanted the watch back, but he had lost the glove. He expected Javier to give him the watch back anyway and when he wouldn't, "I hit him."

"It was wrong to hit him, Joey. You should have gone to Socorro. She would have helped you both figure something out."

"I know. I'm sorry."

Carmen knocked on the door. "Susan, you have a call."

When I picked up the phone, Mary said, "Bring him over."

"Joey, I'm taking you to a new foster home. Socorro can't take care of you anymore because you hurt Javier. You can't do things like that."

"Don't be mad, Susan."

I went over and put my arm around his shoulder. "I'm not mad, I'm worried. I care about you. I don't want to see you go from foster home to foster home. I know what a wonderful kid you are."

"I really miss my mom." I knew how he felt.

"I know you do. But you're really going to like Mary and Doug. And guess what?"

"What?"

"You're going to be the only kid there. You'll get sooo much attention." He smiled. "Will you visit me?"

"Of course."

"Okay. Then I'll go."

"Good decision, Joey. Get your stuff. I'm taking you there now. They're waiting for you."

I got to the airport an hour early and paced back and forth as I waited for her plane to land. I felt envious as I watched other people greeting their spouses and lovers with warm hugs and kisses, wishing that we could be as demonstrative in public. When her plane arrived and the passengers started filing out the door, I felt nervous as I searched for her face. It reminded me of the feeling I used to get before we moved in together. I was always afraid that she would change her mind about being with me.

I waved when I saw her. She smiled and walked over to me. I gave her a quick hug. "I'm so glad you're home."

"Me too. Let's get out of here."

The airport was crowded. I went to get the car while she waited for her luggage. When she finally got in, she nearly collapsed in the front seat. "What a hassle," she complained. When I maneuvered my way out of the parking lot, she reached for my hand and squeezed it. "How are you?"

"I'm fine now. How did it go?"

"It went all right. Jenny got her dress and finally decided where she wanted to have the reception. I swear, we must have checked out 30 places. She was so picky!"

"That's not what I meant."

"I know. Can we talk about it later? I'm exhausted."

"It didn't go well, did it?"

"Not now, Susan. We have the whole night."

I didn't push it any further, but it surprised me that she was so evasive. It scared me too. I felt my whole future with her depended on this.

After a minute or two, she started talking about the wedding. "You can't imagine how much all of this is costing my parents. She could probably put a down payment on a house with the money. I'm a little surprised that they're going all out like this. Jenny always told me that she never wanted a big wedding. I think her boyfriend's parents are really pushing for it. They have a very big family. In fact the guest list has twice as many people coming from his family then we do from ours."

I was half listening, but I really didn't care about Jenny's wedding. I just wanted to know how Jenny felt about Kathy and me living together. And, more importantly, how Kathy felt about what Jenny said.

When we finally got in, I said, "Why don't you just relax? I'm making you a special dinner."

"Oh, this I've got to see."

"No, really. I want to do this myself."

"Have you been taking cooking lessons while I've been gone?" she teased. "Well, it's good to see you haven't lost your sense of humor. It's no big deal.

Now get out of the kitchen."

I heard the shower go on as I put the steaks in the broiler. By the time she had finished unpacking, I had everything on the table. I poured two glasses of wine and took one in to her. After she took a sip, she put it down on her dresser. "Come here, so I can say hello properly."

She put her arms around me and kissed me softly on the lips. It made me feel a little better. "Come on, dinner's ready." I had made her favorite meal -- steak, baked potatoes and salad.

"This is perfect. Are you going to spoil me like this every night?"

"I'll never tell. I want to keep you guessing. It's more interesting that way." "You don't have to keep me guessing to be interesting. You're already the most interesting person I've ever met. Don't you know that?" After a long silence, I said," Are you ready to talk about it?"

"Susan, it was horrible." She started to cry. "She said I would surely go to hell if I didn't leave you and go back to my Christian way of life."

"Oh, Kathy. You don't believe that, do you?"

"Most of the time I don't. But there's still a little part of me that feels really tortured."

I went around to her side of the table and put my arms around her shoulder, pulling her head to my breast. She was sobbing now. I held her for a long time. At that moment, I hated Jenny. What a righteous, ignorant, little bitch! I didn't share my thoughts with Kathy. Instead, I did what I always did when she was upset. I tried to cheer her up.

"You know, if you end up in hell, I'll be there too. At least we'll still be together."

"You can't joke about this. Don't you realize how serious this is to me?" she snapped.

I felt foolish. "I'm sorry. I just hate to see you so upset." "Well, maybe you won't have to."

"What do you mean?"

"Susan, sometimes I do think about leaving. I just don't know if I can handle this."

"What? I can't believe that." Was my worst fear really coming true?

"Don't get upset. I'm not going to do it. I just don't know how to resolve these feelings. I love you, but I feel like I've ruined my life and in the process, I've ruined yours too."

"You haven't ruined my life. You've made my life. I didn't have a life before I met you."

"Of course you did. And so did I. While I was home, I remembered what that life was like. I watched my parents. I watched Jenny and her boyfriend making plans for their future, talking about having children. What kind of future do we have? Hiding out in bars? Being isolated in our apartment? What kind of a life is that?"

"It's a beautiful life if you're in it. Don't you feel that way about me?" "Yes. But I'm not sure it's enough."

I walked back to the other side of the table and looked down at my half-eaten dinner. "Well, so much for spoiling you. Do you want this? I'm not really hungry anymore."

"I didn't want to have this conversation tonight. I'm sorry." "We keep apologizing to each other, don't we?"

"Be honest, Susan. It's been difficult for you too."

"You're right. It's difficult to live each day wondering if you're still going to be here. I'm getting tired of it."

"I don't blame you. I'm sick of it myself."

"This may not be the right time to talk about it, but at some point you're going to have to decide if you want to plan a future with me"

"That's the problem. We can't get married. We can't have children. What do we have to plan?"

"Lots of straight couples don't have children." "But I want children, don't you?"

"Not more than I want you."

"Susan, you say that now, but are you really going to feel this way in two or three years?"

"I don't know, but if you want to leave, then leave already. Quit torturing us like this." I got up from the table and went to my room, slamming the door behind me. I was shaking, not knowing what I felt more, anger or fear. I waited, hoping she would follow me, but she didn't. When I couldn't stand it anymore, I went out to apologize. She wasn't in the living room or kitchen, so I knocked on her bedroom door. When she didn't answer, I opened it slowly, but she wasn't there. I ran to the front window. Her car was gone. "Oh my God. What have I done?"

I was frantic. I paced up and down the street until it got dark. Then I went back inside. All I could do was wait. I thought that she probably went to John's house, but I didn't want to call her there. I didn't know what I would say.

Finally, I heard the key in the door. I walked over and opened it. We just stood there looking at each other. Then I pulled her inside.

She spoke first. "I can't leave you."

"Kathy, I don't want you to leave. I didn't mean it." We hugged each other and I kissed the tears from her face.

"Let's not talk anymore tonight. Let's just love each other."

"Yes," I said softly as we walked into the bedroom. Neither one of us said another word the rest of the night.

When we got to work for the next morning, I called Mary to check on Joey. "I think he's starting to come around. I actually caught him smiling yesterday."

"That's good, Mary. I knew you would be able to help him. I'm going to pick him up at school and bring him home, so I'll see you later."

When he saw me, he smiled. What are you doing here?" "Oh, come on. Admit it. You're glad to see me."

He laughed. "Okay. I'm glad to see you."

"You look good, Joey. I think your new home agrees with you. How 'bout a hamburger?"

"No thanks. Mary's cooking meatloaf tonight. It's my favorite." "Well, come on. I'll take you home."

As we drove, he chatted away about all the things Doug was teaching him. "Last night I helped him change the spark plugs in his car."

"That's great, Joey," I said, almost automatically.

"What's wrong, Susan? You seem sad." He was very perceptive. "Can I help?"

"What is this? A role reversal?"

"You help me. Why can't I help you?"

"You do help me. Just seeing you smile helps me." "Are you having boyfriend problems?"

"You don't give up, do you?" "Well, are you?"

"No. I don't have a boyfriend. Maybe you can be my boyfriend."

"Be serious. You're too old for me. Why would I want to be with an old woman?"

He was smiling. I knew he was teasing me. I laughed. "You're too much."

When we got to the house, I went in with him to say hi to Mary and to let her know what a great job she and Doug were doing with Joey. He almost seemed happy again.

As I turned to leave, Joey said, "Remember, Susan. The pain you feel now will heal, and then you'll be able to go on with your life."

"I can't believe you remembered that." "I remember everything you tell me." "Thanks. I needed that."

"I know."

CHAPTER TWENTY-TWO

WE BEGAN SPENDING MORE TIME apart. We didn't plan it that way. It just happened naturally. I joined a summer softball league; she started taking some classes at the university. I spent a lot of time with Lynn and Dennis; she spent more time with John and Ann. We tried to pretend things between us weren't strained, but it got more difficult every day.

Lynn and Dennis had their baby, a little boy they named James. We both went to the hospital the night he was born. I promised Lynn I would be there. As much as she loved Dennis, she still counted on me for emotional support. At first, Kathy seemed to resent it. She thought that Lynn would want me back. But now, it didn't bother her. She even encouraged me to spend more time with her.

When Lynn and Dennis started going out again, they would leave Jimmy with us. We were the only people they trusted to take care of him. I loved watching Kathy hold and cuddle him. She'd smile and coo at him for hours. It was wonderful to see her genuinely happy.

Most of our conversations centered on work, but even there, we rarely saw each other. Kathy had been promoted to clinical director for the Southern California district, and spent a lot of time at our other branches. On most days we didn't even drive in together, as we both needed a car for home and office visits.

I rarely saw Teresa, but Mindy kept me up to date on her progress. She was having some problems in school at first, but Betty spent hours with her every night, helping her catch up to her appropriate grade level. She was in Jr. High School now and started going to dances and parties. All in all, she was adjusting very well.

I saw Joey every week. We did everything we could to try to find a close relative, but nothing turned up. Both of Mona's parents had died. Joey remembered having an aunt but he hadn't seen her in years and didn't know her last name. The police had searched their files and had come up empty. Joey didn't seem to mind. Doug and Mary were crazy about him and showered him with the attention he had craved so much from his mother. He was always glad to see me. My visits with him were a precious part of my life.

We were sitting on the patio, enjoying the cool, night breeze after a scorching hot day. We hadn't talked about our relationship since the night she got back from Kansas.

"You know, we can't go on like this," I said. "We have to talk about it." "I know. I just don't know how."

"Let's get some help. One of the women on the team gave me the name of a therapist who specializes in gay relationships."

"You want to see a gay therapist?"

"Kathy, isn't that the issue? Who would understand more? I'm certainly not going to go to a Christian counselor."

She laughed. "You're right. But I don't know." "You don't know what?"

"I just don't want you to expect too much."

"Look. Whatever way it goes, it has to be better than this. Look at us! We're miserable together."

She looked surprised. "My God, Susan. Is that what I've done to you?" "You didn't do anything to me. For god sakes, you feel guilty enough. You don't need to take on more."

"I just wish I could be different for you." "You are who you are. Please, will you go?" "Yes. Make the appointment."

We met at her office. She smiled warmly when she greeted us. "Hi. You must be Kathy and Susan. I'm Gloria." She was a stunning woman in her mid-forties. Not at all what either one of us expected. You'd never know she was gay. I think that made Kathy feel a little more comfortable. And it made me realize that Kathy wasn't the only one with stereotypical views of lesbians.

"Well, how can I help you today?"

"We're at an impasse in our relationship," I began. "And we don't know how to talk about it. We love each other but I think we're both terrified that we have some issues that we can't resolve."

Kathy took my hand. "I think what Susan means is that I have issues. She's wonderful. That's what makes this so difficult. I'm so torn between my love for her and my inability to accept a gay lifestyle."

"I see. Do you believe that you're gay?"

"Well, yes. Otherwise, I don't think I could feel this way about her."

"And, if you break up, what then?" Kathy looked at me. "Don't look at Susan for the answer. I'm asking you."

"I don't know."

"Well, let's start from the beginning."

We told her how we met and fell in love. When we finished, she pointed out how we both ignored Kathy's ambivalent feelings and got involved in spite of it. Then she asked us both if we wanted things to get better between us. I nodded yes. Kathy said, "I don't know."

"Then, I don't think I can help you," she said sadly. "For any relationship to survive, both partners have to be committed; especially in a gay relationship. With all the rejection that you'll have to face daily, you have to be able to count on your partner for the love and support that you need. I don't know how your relationship can survive without a total commitment from both of you."

I knew she was right, but it didn't keep me from feeling extremely disappointed. I just wasn't ready to give up on this relationship!

She got up and shook our hands. "Good luck to both of you."

Kathy walked out the door first. Suddenly she stopped in her tracks. "What's wrong?" I followed her eyes to the corner of the room. A familiar figure looked up from her magazine. It was Betty. I pushed Kathy ahead, waving briefly.

When we got back in the car, I said, "Don't worry, she's not going to tell anyone."

"You don't seem surprised, Susan."

"I'm not. I've suspected Betty was gay from the beginning." "And you didn't say anything?"

"What should I have said? And what would you have done with the information?"

"I would have made damn sure that the whole staff knew so we could have made a better decision about her."

I was shocked. "How can you say that! What difference does it make that she's gay as far as her ability to be a parent? Do you think she's inferior? Do you think that gay people make bad parents? Is that what you think about me? About us?" I was furious!

"Well, no."

"No," I shouted. "What a hypocrite you are! Don't you understand? It's people just like you that keep people like us in the closet. My God, Kathy, I never realized how fucked up you really are." As soon as I said it, I regretted it. "Oh God. I'm sorry. I wasn't thinking. I didn't mean that."

She didn't say anything. She just looked straight ahead. I reached for her hand, but she pulled it away.

"Kathy, please, don't do this."

"Now maybe you'll understand how difficult this is for me. It's schizophrenic! Sometimes I really believe I'm going crazy." For the first time, I really understood how conflicted she was.

"I don't think you're going crazy. But, I'm sure that it feels terrible for you to be so confused. I'm truly sorry for what I said."

"But you're right, Susan. Here I am, ready to cry 'Queer' about someone who's probably struggled as much as I have with these issues."

She paused. "Why isn't it a struggle for you?"

"I just don't think about it that much. I focus on what I have rather than what I don't."

"Do you think you can teach me how to do that?"

"I've been trying. Can't you tell?" I was starting to feel a little calmer.

She laughed. "Susan, I know you won't believe this, but I truly wish I could just love you and screw the rest of the world."

"People can't hurt you if you won't allow it. But unless you feel good about who you are, how can you expect other people to accept it?"

"Well, you were right about the counseling. It sure got us talking to each other." We both laughed. "I actually feel better."

"Really? Will you go back?"

"Probably. But not right away. I think I have some work to do on my own." "Does that mean you're not giving up?"

"I can't. I love you too much."

"What a relief. What are you going to do about Betty?"

"Nothing. Why don't you call her tomorrow and reassure her? You're sure Teresa will be okay there?"

"Absolutely." I took her hand. "I have a great idea." "What?"

"Just trust me. Let me drive." I wouldn't tell her where we were going. When we got close I said, "Close your eyes."

"The last time we did this, you kissed me. This is a long way to drive for a kiss."

We got out of the car. "This is a trust walk. So keep those eyes closed. I promise I'll keep you safe."

I guided her carefully up the incline and when we got to the top, I said, "Open your eyes."

"Oh, Susan! I can't believe you thought of this." We were on top of the hill by John's house.

"Come here." I sat down by the same rock and spread my legs so that she could sit between them. I put my arms around her, just as I did that night. I desperately wanted to get back to where we were. She seemed to sense that.

She spoke first. "Do you think you'd do it all again, knowing how difficult it's been?"

"I don't even have to think about it. Of course." "Even though I'm really fucked up."

I laughed. "That's the best part about you." "Liar!"

"What do you think is the best part about me?" "That you haven't given up on me."

We sat there until the sun set over the water. When we got up, I kissed her. Then we held hands all the way home. And for a short time, we both forgot how painful the past few months had been.

We drove into work together the next morning. I didn't want to leave her out of my sight. I was afraid she'd change her mind. I called Betty.

"Susan, about yesterday..."

"Look, don't worry about it," I assured her. "It's between us. No one else need ever know."

She sounded relieved. "Thanks. It's been a difficult night to say the least." "If it makes you feel any better, I've known since the beginning."

She wasn't surprised. "I thought you did. I wanted to ask you about it, but I couldn't."

I understood. "Does Teresa know?"

"Of course not. But when she's old enough I plan to tell her. Be assured, I'd never do anything to embarrass her or jeopardize the final adoption."

"Kathy feels the same way I do about it. I wanted you to know that too," I said reassuringly.

"I must say, you two look good together." I laughed. "Say hi to Teresa for me."

"I will. And thanks again, Susan. You can't imagine how much better I feel."

When I met Kathy for lunch, she was pleased about Betty. Then she suddenly said, "Susan, let's go away together." "You mean forever?" "No silly. A vacation. Just for a week."

"That sounds wonderful. Can we both be gone at the same time? After all, what would people think?"

"For the first time, I don't care. I've already talked to Dave about it. He said it would be fine." I didn't tell Kathy, but I was sure that Dave had figured out what was going on between us. He was a very sensitive and intuitive man. I was also sure that he didn't have any negative feelings about it. He had always been very warm and supportive toward both of us.

"Well, where do you want to go?"

"Mexico. I've already checked out some places there and Mazatlan sounds terrific. What do you say?"

"I say when do we leave?"

"Saturday. I already made the plane and hotel reservations." I smiled. "You don't mess around, do you?"

"Susan, I want us to go on this trip. We need it. Don't you agree?" Absolutely, I thought. It would be a chance to go where no one knows us and we can just be ourselves.

"Yes. I'll have to go shopping. I don't even have a bathing suit." "I have a feeling you're not going to need a lot of clothes." "Kathy, I like this new you. Do you speak Spanish?"

"I only need to learn one phrase." "Oh yeah, what's that?"

"Te Quiero" "Which means?" "I love you."

CHAPTER TWENTY-THREE

NEITHER ONE OF US HAD been to Mexico before, so we didn't know what to expect. It was mid-August, right at the height of the tourist season, and the airport was crowded with people when we landed. We had difficulty getting a cab, so Kathy used an old trick she learned from her father. She pulled out the Hotel's brochure and waved it around. We were told that it was a forty-minute drive from the airport and would make someone a good fare. It worked. We threw our suitcases in and were on our way.

We were astounded by the obvious poverty in the small towns as we passed. Most of the houses were little wooden shacks of one or two rooms. Children on the streets were begging for money from the few tourists who had come to get a closer look. We were upset by these terrible living conditions, but were determined not to let anything interfere with this time together.

When we got to our hotel, we were drenched with perspiration from the hot temperature and high humidity. The hotel was old and quite small, but it was clean. The desk clerk spoke enough English to make the registration process go quickly. The room was lovely, painted in light blue with a large balcony overlooking the ocean. The beach was lined with pure, white sand and the water was so clear that you could see a sandbar about thirty yards offshore. "Oh, it's perfect," Kathy cried, throwing open the balcony doors and leaning over the side. "Come look, Susan."

She took my hand. "I'm having a wonderful time already! Just think.

We don't have to worry about running into people we know for eight whole days. And I have you all to myself."

"Mmm, the Mexican air must agree with you. I've never seen you look so relaxed. You're just really beautiful."

"So, what do you want to do first?" I looked at the bed and raised my eyebrows. "That's exactly what I was thinking."

We found out the name of a good restaurant from the desk clerk. It was still light outside. There were young Mexican men every few yards with suitcases full of watches and jewelry baiting the tourists with promises of unbelievable bargains. "Lady, lady. Over here," one of them called as we crossed the street. His suitcase was full of beautiful turquoise jewelry. "I sell it to you cheap." Kathy picked up a necklace for a closer look. "Isn't it beautiful, Susan?"

"How much?" I asked. "Twenty-five dollars."

I took out my wallet. Kathy stopped me. "No, no. Half the fun of buying it is bargaining with them. Watch."

I watched with amusement as she talked the young boy into selling the necklace to me for nineteen dollars. "You're really good at that. Maybe you missed your calling," I joked as I handed the boy a twenty dollar bill.

We laughed loudly as we walked away. Kathy admired her new necklace. "Thank you. I love it." We had a wonderful time on the way to the restaurant, looking at the stores and watching the people. Everyone seemed so relaxed and happy. Strangers smiled at us and said hello as we walked arm-in-arm down the narrow street.

We ordered margaritas before dinner and toasted our newfound freedom. We sat in a booth on the same side of the table and held hands. No one stared or made us feel different. "We should just move here, Kath. That would solve everything."

She smiled. "I'm so glad we're here together. No matter what happens, I'll never forget being here with you."

We spent the next few days relaxing by the pool during the day, having long, intimate dinners in the evening and making love late into the night. "This is almost more wonderful than that first week we spent together at your house. You were so right to come here. I couldn't imagine being any happier," I whispered as we laid together in each other's arms. "I can't believe that just last week we were ready to pack it in. I don't know how I could have ever considered that."

"I've always believed that if you and I didn't have to deal with the prejudices of the rest of the world, we could work the other things out," she said softly.

"But if we're this happy, why do you even care what other people think?" "You know, the only answer I can come up with is that's who I am. I'm trying to change. I want to change. I know I have to change if we're going to stay together."

"I'll make you change," I said playfully, tickling her. She laughed and tried to catch my arms to make me stop. I pushed her down and grabbed both of her arms by her wrists and kneeled above her. Then I put my face so close to hers that her lips were nearly touching mine. "You know you couldn't live without this." I kissed her passionately; then pulled away. "If you want more, you have to promise you'll never leave me." She lifted her head up to reach my lips, but I pulled away just slightly. "Promise me." She looked at me, helplessly, dropping her head back on the pillow. I followed, keeping my lips just above hers. "Do you promise?"

"Susan..."

"No, just promise."

"I promise. I promise," she whispered, so softly that I could barely hear. When I let go of her arms, she wrapped them around me pulling me closer. Then I kissed her again and again, until we became one, clinging to each other in that one moment of total commitment.

Before we drifted off to sleep, she whispered, "You sure drive a hard bargain."

"Only when I'm sure about what I want."

"I think that's what I admire most about you." "You mean that I'm sure about loving you."

"No. Not just that. You're sure about yourself. You're really a much stronger person than I am. You have confidence in your decisions."

"I always thought you were the confident one."

"I can put up a good front. With you, Susan, it's real. Everything about you is real."

"You won't forget your promise, will you?" "Let's go to sleep now."

"Kathy. You will try?" "Yes, I'll try."

The next morning the hotel was taking several guests on a tour that ended with a boat ride to a little island about twenty miles off shore. We decided to go. We heard there was a nude beach on the island and we both wanted to see it. Two women in their early twenties were among the other guests. They were both attractive and they were obviously in love. Kathy watched them intently as we ate our breakfast. "See, not all lesbians are old and ugly," I said when I saw what she was looking at. "Let's go over and introduce ourselves. It would be fun to hang out with them."

Their names were Debbie and Sandy. They told us that they had been together for three months. Sandy was a student at the University of Arizona and Debbie was a waitress at the local restaurant. They asked us how we met and how long we had been together. It was the first time we shared our relationship with other people together. It was wonderful listening to Kathy talk so openly about her feelings for me. Every once in a while she would reach over and take my hand for a moment or two, then drop it quickly when she realized what she was doing. The three of us would laugh. Finally, she just said, "Oh screw it," and held my hand the rest of the way.

The island was beautiful. It was hard to believe that we were just a few miles from the most impoverished conditions I had ever seen. The rest of the people from the tour walked into town, while the four of us decided to stay at the nude beach. Except for us, it was totally deserted. We waded in the shallow water, which was clear and warm, and splashed each other like four little children.

"Let's go in," Sandy suddenly shouted, unbuttoning her blouse, and then taking off her bikini top. She ran up to the beach and pulled down her shorts and bikini bottoms. Then she came racing back. "Come on, you guys, it's great."

Kathy and Debbie ran back to the beach and stripped, while I just stood there, frozen. "Susan's a little bashful," Kathy teased, trying to encourage me to remove my clothes. Then they dove under the water, loving the total freedom of being nude in the ocean. What the hell, I thought, racing back to the beach. I suddenly stopped in my tracks. Two young Mexican men were standing by our clothes, watching. Then they started walking toward me. "Come on, Susan," Kathy called. Then she saw them. In a second, all three of them were swimming towards me, screaming. I backed up to where the water touched my waist to meet them.

"What should we do?" I was terrified. Debbie shouted, "What do you want?"

"We want to fuck you," one of them shouted back, making lewd gestures. "Oh my god," Sandy kept whispering. "Oh my god."

Suddenly, Kathy stepped forward. "Get out of here, you perverts," she screamed, waving her hands wildly. "Our friends will be back any minute." She was walking toward them, shouting loudly as she moved. I started mimicking her screams.

Then Debbie screamed, "You bastards, leave us alone." Then Sandy joined in. As we closed in on them, they looked totally confused.

They laughed nervously and whispered something to each other, then turned and started walking away. We waited until they were out of sight.

After we calmed down, I looked at Kathy. "My hero! You were so brave!"

Debbie chimed in. "Oh my god, I was so scared. You really ran them off. I don't know what would have happened if you weren't here."

I started chanting "KA-THY, KA-THY." They joined in. Kathy just beamed.

We were glad to see the other guests coming back from town, partly because we knew we were safe and partly because we had such a great story to tell.

When we finally got back to our hotel and said goodbye to Sandy and Debbie, I just hugged Kathy. "You were wonderful. You saved the day."

"I don't know where that came from, Susan. I just knew I wasn't going to let them hurt you no matter what."

"You're a real keeper, sweetheart." We walked up the stairs to our room and closed the door. "Now I can thank you properly for saving my life. You know what they say. Once you save somebody's life, you own it."

"Oh really. Does that mean you have to listen to me from now on?" "Yes."

"And you'll do what I say?" "Yes."

"Then, get over here."

I felt very sad on our last day. I know that she did too. But we didn't talk about it. We didn't want to ruin the time we had left.

We spent the morning in bed, and then decided to take a taxi to the other side of town for lunch. We sat next to each other, holding hands, whispering words of commitment and promise that we both knew would be hard to keep. We wandered through the shops, buying small souvenirs for our friends and coworkers at home. Then we sat on the beach and watched the sunset before having a light dinner at the hotel and going up to our room. We sat on the balcony for a long time without talking. She broke the silence. "It was a

wonderful vacation, Susan. I'm so glad we have it to remember."

"I don't think I'll ever forget the sight of you, naked as a jaybird, chasing those guys away. I laugh every time I think about it."

"Now, now. Remember, I saved your life."

"In more ways than one," I said seriously. "I don't know what I did that was so wonderful to ever deserve you. No matter what happens, I'll never be sorry that we loved each other."

"Nor will I, my love. Promise me something."

"Anything."

"That you'll always stay as open and as vulnerable as you are right now. Don't ever change that. No matter how much pain there is in the world, don't ever change that."

"Let's go in."

We undressed slowly, as if we were trying to memorize the moment. No matter how many times I saw her body, I still marveled at the beauty of it. We made love passionately, clinging to each other, not wanting the night to end. It was almost as if we both knew it would be the last time.

CHAPTER TWENTY-FOUR

"DOES IT FEEL GOOD TO be home?" she asked, after we unpacked and showered. Not waiting for an answer, she picked up the phone. "I need to let my parents know that I'm back. Hi mom," she said cheerfully seconds later. She was silent for several minutes, listening intently. Her face went white and her eyes filled with tears. When she hung up the phone, she said, almost in a daze, "My God. My father had a heart attack yesterday. He's in intensive care. I have to go home right away."

"Oh, Kathy."

"Can you call the airlines? I have to pack." It was 2:30. I got her on a flight that left at 4:45.

"Can you take me to the airport, Susan? We have to leave right away."

When we got there, she jumped out of the car. "I'm going to park," I called out to her. "I'll meet you at the gate."

"But if I miss you "

"You won't miss me!"

The parking lot was crowded and it took longer than I thought. I raced to the gate. She was already walking toward the plane. "Kathy," I yelled. "Kathy, wait!" She looked around and saw me. I tried to get by the stewardess taking tickets, but she stopped me.

"Hey, you can't go beyond this point." I broke away. "Hey, come back!"

I ran up to her, hugging her tightly. "Kathy, I pray that your dad will be okay." People were staring at us. I let her go and touched her face. "You won't forget your promise, will you?"

"No, honey. I won't forget. I'll call you tonight. I love you," she whispered. She turned and walked up the stairs. At the top, she turned around and waved. Then she disappeared into the plane.

The stewardess just glared at me as I walked back out. "Sorry," I said. But she didn't answer.

It had all happened so quickly. I kept remembering what happened the last time she went to Kansas. I didn't want to go through that again. I cried all the way home.

I tried to read, but I couldn't concentrate. When she finally called, it was a very brief conversation. Her father's condition was critical, but he was out of imminent danger for the time being. "He's hooked up to so many machines and looks so helpless. It's just hard to see him this way."

"You know I'm not a religious person, but I'm praying for him. Are you all right?"

"Yes. John and Ann are here, so it's pretty crowded in the house. I've barely had a minute to myself. Anyway, I'll call you in a few days."

"You take care of yourself. Don't worry about anything here." "I won't. I love you, Susan."

"I love you too."

I didn't ask her how she felt about Ann being included as part of their family when she couldn't even talk to her parents about the person that she loved. It made me feel very sad.

Over the next few days, I tried to keep busy. Some of the women on the softball team invited me to join them for dinner. I spent more time with Lynn and Dennis, and, of course, Jimmy. My first day back at work was difficult. Everyone asked where Kathy was. Apparently, Dave hadn't told them about her father, so I assumed she didn't want people to know. Steve joked, "Maybe she met some rich guy down in Mexico and decided to stay." What a jerk! I thought. I had to get out of there. Making a home visit to see Joey was the perfect excuse to duck out. I had really missed him.

He was playing in the front yard when I drove up. He looked like he had grown two inches and his hair was getting longer. He was losing his cute little baby face and was turning into a handsome boy.

"Hi, good lookin'," I said as he came running up for a hug. "How was Mexico, Susan? Did you bring me back anything?"

"Well, as a matter of fact, I did," I said, handing him a small box. When he opened it, the look of disbelief on his face was priceless.

"Oh my God, a watch!"

"And you'd better not trade it away." "I can't believe you got me a watch!"

"It was fun picking it out. Kathy helped me. Do you like it?" "It's beautiful. Thank you." He was beaming.

"I'm going in to talk to Mary. Want to come?"

"In a minute." He ran off, shouting, "Hey, Bobby. Look at my new watch." "Hi Mary." She gave me a warm hug. We had grown quite close and sometimes talked for hours over coffee about Joey, Teresa, and the plans she and Doug had for the future. It came as no surprise when she brought up wanting to adopt Joey. I had brought the subject up in a staff meeting weeks ago. I was emphatic about not moving him. And this time I was prepared to argue the point, even if it cost me my job. Unlike Teresa, I really didn't think Joey could handle losing Doug and Mary. To my surprise, the whole staff supported me. It made me feel good about all of them.

"I know that you and Doug are crazy about him and I don't think we could ever find him better parents. I've already talked it over with the staff and they all agree. We've just been waiting for you to bring it up."

She laughed. "We've been afraid to bring it up. We thought you'd really start to wonder about us wanting to adopt both of the kids you placed with us. We remember you warning us in the training classes that the hardest part of the process would be getting attached to the kids and then having to let go. I guess we're not really good at the letting go part."

"Well, that's lucky for Joey. You'll have to go through the screening process again. It's a little different for adoptive parents, but since we have a lot of the information, I don't think it will be that difficult or take too long."

"Thank you, Susan." "Does Joey know?"

"No. We didn't want to get his hopes up until we were sure it would be possible. Do you want to tell him?"

"Well, I can feel him out, but I think you and Doug should have the pleasure of breaking the news."

At that moment, Joey came racing in the door.

"Mary, look what Susan gave me." He pushed his wrist into her face.

"Joey. It's beautiful." She turned to me. "That was wonderful of you to get him that."

"Are you staying for lunch?" Joey asked.

"I really have to get back to the office. Want to walk me to my car?" "Sure."

"Bye Mary. We'll be in touch."

Joey took my hand as we walked out. "So, you seem pretty happy here." "I guess so."

"What do you mean, I guess so," giving him a pat on his head. "Well, I don't want to tell you I'm too happy."

"Why?"

"Cause then you won't come to see me anymore."

"But if you're really happy, you won't need to see me as much." "I'll always want to see you. You're my best friend."

I stopped and hugged him. "That's the nicest thing any kid has ever said to me. Look, Joey, I don't want you to worry about that right now. I don't want you to worry about anything. You just enjoy every day."

"Okay. Thank you for the watch, Susan."

"It was my pleasure." It was truly wonderful to see him so happy.

During the next few weeks, Kathy called three times. The first time she told me that her father was still in critical condition and that she was going to stay for a few more weeks.

"My mother needs me, Susan. John and Ann had to go back and Jenny works all day. I just can't leave her alone right now."

"I understand, honey. Would you like me to come there and be with you?" "I'd love it. But you can't."

"But Ann was there." "That's different."

"Why?" I probably shouldn't have pushed it. It wasn't really her fault. "Susan, I get your point." She paused. "I can't do this with you now. Please understand."

Her second call came four days later. "It looks like dad is going to make it. His heart is stronger, and he's sitting up now for short periods of time."

"That's wonderful, Kathy. Does that mean you'll be coming home soon?" "I'm going to stay another week. Mom may need some help for a while when we get dad home. How are things going back there?"

"Besides missing you like crazy, we were right about Doug and Mary. They want to adopt Joey."

"That's great. How did he take it?"

"I wasn't there when they told him, but Mary said he was ecstatic." "That's wonderful. Really wonderful."

"You sound tired."

"Yeah. It's been pretty exhausting. When I get home I'll probably want to sleep for a week."

"I know how to keep you awake."

She didn't laugh. "I'll call you soon, Susan. I have to run." I stood by the phone for about two minutes after she hung up. I thought for sure she'd call back and apologize for being so abrupt. But she didn't. I made up all kinds of excuses -- her mother was in the room or she was calling from the hospital -- but I knew her doubts about our relationship were starting again.

The third time she called, her father was home. "That's great. So are you coming home soon?"

"Yes. Soon. Susan, I think I should tell you something before I get there." From the sound of her voice, I knew it wasn't good news. "Go on."

"I ran into an old High School boyfriend at the hospital. He's a doctor here. We had coffee a few times and, well, he's asked me out."

I was stunned. "You're not going, are you?" "Yes. I am."

"Kathy"

"Please don't try to talk me out of it. I've made up my mind." "Made up your mind about what?"

"To go out with him."

"Why don't you just tell me everything?" "I like him. I like him a lot."

"Well, have a good time then." "Susan, I don't want to hurt you."

"Then why are you going?"

She was silent. Then she said, "Let's talk about this when I get home." "I know," I said coldly, "You have to run."

"See you soon," she said and hung up. As many times as I thought about the worst thing that could have happened when she went to Kansas, I never imagined this. How could she do this to me? I was devastated! I had to talk to someone. I called the only person I could think of that would understand how I felt. I called Gloria.

"Thank you for seeing me on such short notice,"

"Are you and Kathy not together anymore? I expected to see both of you." "She's back in Kansas. Her father had a heart attack."

"Oh, I'm sorry. Is he going to be all right?" "She thinks so."

"But you're not, are you?"

"No." I told her what had happened since the last time we were there. When I got to the part about Kathy going out with her high school boyfriend, I started to cry. "I just don't understand how she could do this to me?"

"Is it that you don't understand or you don't want to understand?"
"What do you mean?"

"Susan, you know that Kathy has struggled with this relationship since the beginning. Maybe she's just tired of the struggle." "But, in Mexico…"

"Mexico was a beautiful fantasy. It was a place where the two of you were anonymous. The people there couldn't hurt you, so you could enjoy each other the way it should always be. For eight lovely days she was able to run away from all of the pressures, even the ones she has inside of herself. That was a wonderful gift that she gave you."

"But I don't want it to end."

"I know. I don't think she does either. You know, I think you're strong enough to follow your heart. I'm not sure about Kathy."

"So what should I do?"

"Well, what are your choices?"

"I don't have any, really. I've been letting her make all of the decisions." "We always have choices, Susan. Sometimes, we just don't want to look at them."

"You're saying I could leave. Is that what you think I should do?"

"I would never tell you what to do." She may not have said it, but I knew she thought it!

"I don't know why I bothered to come here." I said angrily.

"Maybe you're just not ready to look at your choices. When you are, I'll be here."

I was embarrassed. "I didn't mean to get angry at you." "I know. Who are you angry at?"

"It's pretty obvious."

"Susan, it feels to me like you're in a struggle for Kathy's soul. I know you don't want to give up, but you must be terrified at times that you're going to lose the battle."

I started to cry again. I could never put it into words, but that's exactly the way I felt. "When is she coming back?"

"Probably not for another week, at least."

"So you have some time to think about things." "Yes, I guess I do."

CHAPTER TWENTY-FIVE

KATHY CALLED A FEW DAYS later to let me know that she'd be back at the end of the week. It felt like she had been gone for years, especially after she told me about her old boyfriend. At times, I was terrified she wouldn't come back at all.

She smiled and waved when she saw me. She looked tired. Her face was pale and drawn. Her hair was tied with a rubber band at her neck. Her clothes looked dirty and wrinkled.

"I'm so glad to see you here," she said softly as she gave me a warm hug. "I wasn't sure you would come."

Well, at least she doesn't take me for granted. "Where else would I be? I'm glad you're back."

On the drive home, she talked about how rough this ordeal had been on her mother and how glad she was that she could be there to help her. Then she talked about how much alike they were. "I really got to know her woman to woman. I don't think she's ever shared so much about herself, not even with my father. She's a very spiritual person and has a deep faith in God. She's also very caring, and worries that she doesn't do enough for people, even though she goes overboard to help everyone."

"Gee, that does sound familiar," I tried not to sound sarcastic.

"Yeah. And she's really hung up on what people think about her. She wants them to think the best. It was so interesting to talk to her about all these things, Susan. I never realized how much of her personality she passed down to me. It really helped me understand myself a lot better."

I tried to act interested. "I'm glad, Kath. I know how important that is to you." I wanted to ask if her mother had a lesbian lover before she settled down and got married and raised a family. Then I'd be convinced that they were alike! "And your dad? How's he doing?"

"He's much better. When I left he was already walking around the block three or four times a day. His doctor thinks he'll be back to work in a month or two."

She was silent for a few minutes. Then suddenly she grabbed my hand. "Susan, I'm so sorry that I hurt you."

"You know, Kathy, we've had this conversation so many times that I've practically memorized it. I know that you didn't mean it. I'm not angry. Really I'm not."

"What are you feeling then?" "Sad. Just really, really sad."

"Susan, please believe me. That just breaks my heart."

"So where do we go from here, Kath? Or do we go anywhere?"

"Well, you'll be glad to know that it's not going to work out with him. He had a little secret of his own. He's married!"

"Is that the only reason that it won't work out?" Now I was starting to feel angry.

"You know it's not."

"No I don't. I don't understand why you would go out with him in the first place."

"Susan, I was getting a lot of pressure from my family. How could I tell them the real reason I didn't want to go out with him?"

"Why did you have to give them a reason at all? Couldn't you have just said no and left it at that?"

She didn't answer. We drove the rest of the way in silence.

She went right to her room. When I heard the shower go on, I started dinner. I was sitting at the table when she came out to join me.

"Susan, I want us to repair this. Can't we try?"

"I want that too. More than anything." I paused. "I want to know what happened. Tell me about it."

"There's really nothing to tell. It was just one date."

"Don't be naïve. You know it was much more than that. I want you to be honest with me. Did you kiss him?"

"Susan, don't."

"Look. I'm not asking you because I'm a pervert and want to know all the little sordid details. I'm asking if you were sexually attracted to a man. Don't you think I have a right to know that?"

"Okay, yes. I kissed him." "Did you like it?"

"Yes."

"And then what?"

"That's all. He just stopped. That's when he told me he was married."

"Did you want to stop?"

She just looked at me with this helpless, guilty look on her face. "Never mind. I know the answer."

I got up from the table with tears streaming down my face. She came over to me quickly and put both of her arms around me.

"I'm so sorry. Please forgive me." In a moment she began to cry. We just stood there, holding each other.

When I gained some composure, I said, "I know that you love me, Kathy. I don't think I could ever express in words how much that has meant to me. I'd like nothing more than to live happily ever after with you. But I know that's a fairy tale." I paused. "I don't think we're going to make it together, Kath."

"Let's not talk about it anymore tonight. Let's just sleep on it."

"Okay. But until we decide what we're going to do, I think we should sleep in our own rooms. We've always used sex to keep us together. Let's see if we have anything besides that going for us." I knew that hurt her. And I knew it wasn't true. We had a lot going for us. But I needed her to say it.

"You've changed while I was gone, Susan. You've really changed."

"I think I've grown up a little. At least I hope so. It's about time, isn't it?" I hesitated. "I saw Gloria a few times. She helped me sort some things out."

"Oh. Well, I'm exhausted. Are you sure this is what you want?"

"Absolutely not!" We smiled at each other for the first time. I kissed her on the cheek. "See you in the morning." I felt lonelier that night in my bed than I had the whole time Kathy was gone.

I met Lynn for lunch the next day. She chattered on about Jimmy and all the new things he was learning to do. "The other day he got into one of the cupboards, the one that I keep all my spices in. Well, the next thing I knew, he was sitting there with flour all over him and all over the floor. It was so darn cute, that I couldn't get mad at him. But he's getting to be a real handful. I have to watch him every second."

"Can you use some help?" "What do you mean?"

"I'm thinking of leaving Kathy, or at least separating for a while. Do you think I could stay with you and Dennis until I figure out what I'm going to do?"

"Oh Susan. I thought things were going really well."

"There are times when things between us are wonderful. But other times are really painful. Kathy still vacillates back and forth. When she was in Kansas, she went out with her high school boyfriend. I was devastated. I just don't know if she'll ever commit and I don't know how long I can tolerate her pushing me away every time we seem to make progress getting closer."

"I'm so sorry, Susan. Of course you can stay with us as long as you like." "Thanks. And thanks for not saying I told you so. How are you and Dennis doing? I've been so involved in my own drama, I've been neglecting you again."

"I understand. Things are really okay. Oh, I have my moments of wanting to pack my bags and leave him; he can be so exasperating at times. But he's a good man and really loves me and Jimmy. I don't think

I could find anyone better, except you, of course.

I laughed. "I've often wondered if you ever think of that conversation we had. It seems like so long ago now."

"I remember every word." She smiled. "Heck, you're the only person who ever rejected me."

The next few weeks were strained, to say the least. We continued sleeping in different rooms, but we were trying very hard to find common ground. We usually ate dinner together and then watched TV or played a game.

Kathy tried to put up a good front, but underneath, I knew she was unhappy. The sparkle was gone from her eyes; emotionally, she just wasn't there. Sometimes I would come home to find her crying in her room. I'd just go in and hold her. She'd tell me she was worried about her father. I knew it was a lie, but I didn't confront her. I just didn't see the point anymore.

As for me, I was absolutely miserable. I knew what I could do about it, but I was afraid that if I left, I'd feel worse. So we stayed together. Or I should say, our bodies were together. Emotionally, we couldn't have been farther apart.

I continued to see Gloria. I asked Kathy to go with me, but she refused. I think she was afraid that Gloria would tell us to separate. We both knew that's what we should do, but neither one of us was strong enough to make the move.

One night at dinner, I finally started talking about it. "You know, Kath. I think the reason it's been so hard to let go is because I know how rare it is to find someone like you. I don't think I could ever settle for less and I don't want to be alone."

"I feel the same way about you. I don't want it to end either, but I don't know if I can change enough to make it better."

"Kathy, please forgive me for making things so difficult for you this past month. You were going through a real crisis, and I've been so selfish. All I could think about was me and how lonely I was without you. I was angry that you left me so suddenly after we spent such a wonderful time in Mexico together. What a jerk I've been! I finally realize that all this time I thought I was putting you first. But all along what I've been thinking about is me. I do want you to be happy. I wanted you to be happy with me, but I think I finally understand that I can't make that happen."

"Susan, you've always made me happy. It's me that makes myself unhappy. You've always been so very kind and caring. What makes this so difficult is that I'm not only losing the love of my life, I'm losing my best friend too."

We sat there together for a few more minutes. I felt like I was dying. "Let's get out of here. Come on. Let's go for a walk." As we started up the street, she took my hand and squeezed it. "Do you think we can be friends again after both of us get over the initial pain?"

"I hope so, Kath."

"I guess I knew you weren't going to put up with my ambivalence forever. I just thought we'd have more time."

"Do you think there's a chance your feelings about being gay could ever change? Do you think you could ever feel good about loving me?"

"I don't know, Susan. And it's not fair to you. I know that. It kills me to keep hurting you."

"And the music goes round and round." "What?"

"Did you ever hear that old song? It reminds me of us. It's about how people go through life without ever changing."

"But you've changed, Susan."

"But I'll never change the way I feel about you. I will love you till I die. Even if I find someone else to love, I'll always still love you."

We walked until we were both exhausted. Then we came home and went to our separate rooms.

I couldn't sleep. I had to be with her. Before I could move, the door opened. "Susan? Can I just come in and hold you?" She didn't wait for an answer. In a moment, her arms were wrapped around me. And I felt like I was home.

A few weeks had passed and we were still trying very hard to hold things together. But we both knew it would be extremely difficult to get back to where we were. I'm not even sure she wanted to.

We spent a lot of time at the movies or bowling or riding bikes together. That was easy. It was the time we spent at home together that was the problem. Even though I wanted to, it was very difficult for me to be affectionate with her. I just didn't trust her. I felt that if we got close again, she would do something hurtful to push me away. I couldn't go through it again. I didn't have to explain it to her. She knew. She didn't try to reassure me. I had mixed feelings about that. I was disappointed, but it also made things easier.

She decided to enroll in extra classes at school. Once she started, I hardly saw her. She was taking two science classes and had to spend long hours at the lab. She was thinking of applying to medical school in a few years. I admired her ambition.

One evening, as we were eating dinner, the phone rang. When I answered, a male voice asked for Kathy. As I listened to her talk, I knew this guy was more than a casual friend. She giggled at things he said and she talked in her soft, sexy voice.

"Who was that?" I tried not to sound jealous.

"He's in one of my classes. He was out of town last week and wanted to know if he could borrow my notes."

"Kathy, please don't lie to me."

She didn't look at me. "He wants me to go out with him."

I just looked at her. "Well, I told him no, Susan. Don't look at me like that." "But you want to go, don't you?"

She didn't answer.

"Kathy, I can't do this anymore. I'm going to stay with Lynn and

Dennis for a while. I love you. But I can't stay with you knowing you don't really want to be my partner. I don't blame you. It's not your fault. I just have to do this for me." When I stood up, she touched my arm. "Please. Let me go." I started to cry. "I don't want to do this. I have to leave now."

I raced to my room, grabbed a duffle bag, and threw a few things together. She followed me. "Susan, please don't leave tonight."

I didn't listen. I walked past her to the door. I stopped to look at her one more time. Then I left.

I could hardly see the road ahead through my tears. By the time I got to Lynn's house, I was an absolute basket case. I just laid down on the front seat and sobbed. Lynn knocked on the window. When I unlocked the door, she got in and just held me. "It's okay, Susan. It's okay."

"It's not okay. I don't know if it will ever be again."

CHAPTER TWENTY-SIX

THE NEXT FEW MONTHS WERE a blur. I went through the motions of living my life, but my head just wasn't there. I didn't see much of Kathy at work. She was out of the office most of the time, and when she was there, I would leave and do my home visits. The only time we saw each other regularly was at staff meetings. We both tried to put on a facade that everything was fine -- she was much better at it than I was.

About two weeks after I left, she moved out of our apartment into a one- bedroom unit on the same street. She asked me what I wanted to do with the furniture she had given me. I decided to store it. I didn't have the heart to sell it or give it away.

One day I stopped at the McDonald's for a quick lunch. She was sitting by herself in the corner. "Can I join you?"

"Of course."

I had mixed feelings about how much to share with her. I didn't want her to know how much I was hurting. I didn't want her to feel guilty. And yet, part of me wanted her to know. Part of me wanted her to be as miserable as I was. I was so confused.

"How are you doing?" I finally asked.

"Do you want the polite answer, Susan, or the honest one." "The honest one."

"Shitty. I'm doing shitty." She rarely swore.

"Yeah, me too." It was so pathetic that we both laughed. Finally, I said, "I miss you."

"And I miss you. So what else is new?" Her anger surprised me. "What the hell are you angry about?"

"I'm angry at you, at me, whoever happens to be in the way." "Kathy, we couldn't go on the way it was."

"No. You couldn't."

"Are you saying that you expected me to stick around and watch you go out with men. Every other week you were pushing me away for one reason or another. It was either your family, or religion or God or children or dating. It was driving me crazy!"

"But you knew I had doubts from the beginning, Susan."

"You're right. But I was kidding myself. I did know when we got together that you had negative feelings about two women being together. And I knew you thought it was wrong. But I thought that once you really experienced how wonderful it could be and how happy we were together, you would realize that it's not wrong. I thought you'd feel as lucky that you were with me as I was to be with you. And I thought that you'd be deliriously happy that you were brave enough to risk getting involved. What an ignorant fool I was!" It felt good to finally get that off my chest.

Her voice softened. "Oh Susan. You weren't. I know I was giving you that message. There were times when I thought I could change too. I certainly loved you enough. But I just realized that some things are part of me. I can't change who I am. I can't believe that being with a woman is really okay -- at least not for the rest of my life, no matter how much I love you."

"Do you really think you can be with a man?"

"I know I'll never love a man the way I love you, but I hope I can love one enough. I still want a family. That's all I've ever wanted."

I didn't say anything. I just looked at her. Until that moment I'm not sure I really believed it. "It's really over, isn't it?"

She reached under the table and touched my knee. "Susan, I love you. I'll always love you. But yes, it's really over. I'm not sure I would have ever had the strength to leave you, but I know that was the right decision. I always knew you were the strong one. I think you made the right decision for both of us." She got up and walked out the door.

I saw Gloria later that day.

"I feel like I'm falling apart. I can't sleep. I have to force myself to eat. I can't concentrate on my work. I'm just so miserable. I thought the hardest part would be leaving. I didn't think about what things would be like afterwards. I can't go on like this."

"What are you going to do?"

"I've been thinking of moving away."

"How will that help? You can't escape your feelings."

"I know that, but maybe if I'm in new surroundings... Everything here reminds me of Kathy."

"Have you really thought this through, Susan?" "No. I already told you I can't think straight." "I think I can help you, if you let me."

"Anything. What do you want me to do?"

"Well, I'd like to refer you to a Psychiatrist so that we can get you on some medication. You're in a major depression. That means your brain isn't working right. The medication will help with that."

"Okay." I said it without resisting, but I remembered what medication did to my mother. I was afraid, but I had to trust someone. I thought if I didn't, I would die.

"And I want you to come here two times a week until you're feeling better. You need to talk, Susan. You need to get the pain that's on the inside out of there. If you do, you'll start to feel better. Isn't there anyone else you know that you really enjoy spending time with?"

"Yeah. Joey."

"Well, after we're finished here I want you to go and see him."

The adoption was proceeding well. Since I had done the original screening of Doug and Mary, Dave made an exception and let me keep the case as long as Mindy helped with the paperwork. That meant I could continue seeing Joey every week. I was thankful for that. I don't think I could have handled having to say goodbye to him too.

Everyday was an adventure for him. One day while we were walking together by his house, he screamed, "Oh no. Look at that!" He pointed to a baby bird that had obviously fallen out of its nest. "Poor little thing." The bird was alive, but hardly moving. "We have to help it. You stay here while I get Mary to help." He went running off toward the house, as I hovered over this poor, hurt, little bird.

In a few minutes, Joey came running back with Mary not far behind carrying a shoebox and some paper towels. "Is he still alive, Susan?" he shouted as he got closer. "Over here, Mary." We all huddled around the bird, trying to figure out how to pick it up without hurting it any more than it already was. Joey took a paper towel and carefully wrapped it around the wounded bird, then lovingly picked it up and put it in the shoebox. "You're going to be okay, little fella," he whispered.

For the next few weeks Joey took care of that bird like it was his child. He fed it. He petted it. He even sang to it. When the bird was strong enough to fly, Mary suggested he take the box outside and let it go. "But, how will he find his parents? Who will take care of him? Won't he be lonely?"

Mary didn't know what to say. She looked at me. "You've taken good care of the bird, Joey, and I know that you really love him."

"And he loves me too, Susan."

"I know. But even with all that love, the bird can't be happy unless he's with other birds. He's grateful that you cared for him so much, but you're really different from him. He needs to be with his own kind." My God, I thought. I'm describing Kathy and me. "You have to let him lead the life he was meant to." I started to get into the drama, but even Joey saw through it.

"All right, already. This isn't a soap opera."

As he opened the box, the bird flew out. Joey shouted "Goodbye, my friend. I hope you don't forget me. I'll never forget you." And to me, "Thanks for helping me, Susan."

"Thank you, Joey. You've helped me a lot too."

As the weeks and months passed, I started to feel better. I wasn't happy, but I did feel better. Gloria was a big help. She forced me to look at things more realistically, and I began to develop a healthier perception about things in general. The glass was no longer half empty.

I finally felt ready to call Kathy. I was anxious, but excited, as I dialed the number. "Hi, Kath."

"Well, hi yourself. How are you, Susan?"

"I'm better. Listen, I just wanted you to know that if you still want to be friends, I think I'm ready. I really, really miss talking to you.

"Oh, Susan. That means so much to me. I've really missed talking to you too."

Kathy was dating a man she met at the University. He was an architect in his early thirties. At first, she didn't want to share any of the details about him, but I convinced her that I was really moving on with my life and could handle it.

We began going out for lunch together a few times a month. She'd always ask about my life. Sometimes I made things up, just so she'd think I had gotten past everything. I also wanted to see if she would be jealous. "I met this beautiful woman the other night. She's athletic and smart. We really hit it off. I'm going to meet her later."

"That's wonderful, Susan. I want you to be happy." She'd talk about Peter, the architect, and I'd smile and appear interested. Then I'd go home and cry. By then I had moved into my own apartment. Lynn and Dennis were terrific. They wanted me to stay permanently, but I needed my own space. "We don't want to lose our live-in babysitter," Dennis moaned when I told him I was moving.

"Don't worry. I'll always be around to take care of Jimmy."

I got my bedroom furniture out of storage. I was afraid I might be sad sleeping on it without Kathy, but it didn't bother me.

Once in a while, I would stop at the gay bar for a drink on my way home. One night a woman asked me to dance. I hesitated at first, remembering Lena's agenda. I knew I wasn't ready for anything like that.

"Oh come on," she urged. "It's just a dance."

I followed her to the dance floor. When I put my arm around her neck, she pulled me closer. She led.

"You're a good dancer," I said, trying to make conversation.

"Why are you so nervous?"

"This is new for me. I'm just not sure of myself yet." When the music stopped, she followed me back to the bar.

"You're here alone, aren't you?" I knew what was coming. "Mind if I sit down?"

"No, but I have to leave in a few minutes. I'm meeting someone."

"Someone special?"

"Look, I'm not involved with anyone if that's what you're asking." I was annoyed.

"I'm just trying to be friendly."

"I'm sorry. I didn't mean to snap. I'm just really fragile these days."

"You must have just broken up with someone, huh."

"How did you know that?" I didn't realize I was so transparent.

"I've been there, many times."

I relaxed a little and looked at her for the first time. I longed to talk to someone who would understand how I felt. She seemed genuinely interested, encouraging me to open up and share my feelings.

"That's rough."

"So you've had a similar experience?"

"Well, I've never been involved with a straight woman, but I've certainly had my share of rejections."

"But this isn't about rejection."

"Yeah, of course. You know the best thing to do to forget a lost love?" "What's that?" I waited for her words of wisdom.

"Find another one."

My god, I thought. I finally found someone that was shallower than I am.

Then I corrected myself...than I used to be. Maybe I was getting better! "That's good advice," I answered. "I'll think about it."

She reached for a napkin and wrote something down. "Here's my number. Call me when you're ready."

"Well, I have to run. See ya."

When I got home, I looked at the number. Then I tore it up and threw it in the trash.

I went to court the day the adoption became final. Joey was dressed in a new suit. He looked adorable. "You're so handsome," I said when I saw him. He listened intently as the judge lectured Doug and Mary about the seriousness of the task they were taking on. What a pompous ass, I thought. They probably knew more about parenting and had more love in their hearts for children than anyone I knew. They hardly needed some old judge telling them about the responsibilities of parenthood.

They didn't seem to mind. Joey stood between them, holding their hands and when the judge formally approved the adoption, he hugged them both. "Can I call you mom and dad now?"

"We'd love that, son," Doug answered. It was very touching. Afterwards, we all went out to lunch to celebrate. Mary's mother came to the courtroom. Since Joey had been living there, she had been visiting more often. She was crazy about him and was thrilled to have him as her first grandson.

When the waiter brought dessert, Joey said, "I want to make a speech." We all started to clap. "No. No. You can clap when I'm done."

"When my mom died, I thought my life was over. I didn't think I would ever be happy again. But Susan said I would and she found

Doug and Mary. And now I have wonderful parents and a wonderful grandmother." He looked at me. "And it's because of you, Susan. You've been just terrific, and I'll never, never forget you."

Tears welled up inside. I stood up and hugged him. We both knew that, at least, officially, my visits would stop. We talked about that a lot over the past year. We promised each other that we'd always keep in touch.

I told myself when I left Kathy that I would stay at my job until Joey had a permanent home. The week after the adoption was final, I gave notice. Two weeks later, I was packing my things to leave.

"So, you're really going? Were you going to leave without saying goodbye?"

"This isn't goodbye, Kathy. We'll see each other." "I wonder."

"Look. Besides everything else, you have been the best supervisor I've ever had. I've learned so much from you about relationships, about people. Thank you."

"You made it easy, Susan. Do you need some help with these boxes?" "Sure."

We loaded my things into my car. "Well, I guess this is it. It's hard to believe I'm really leaving. For the last 3 years, this place and the people I've met here have been my whole life."

"What are your plans? I've hardly talked to you."

"I'm going to take some time off from social work. I'd like to do something else for a change."

"I don't blame you. This gets awfully heavy sometimes." "Kathy..."

"You don't have to say anything. I know." She opened her arms. "Goodbye, my friend. I'll be in touch."

"Goodbye, Susan. Good luck."

As I drove away, I looked back one more time, but she had already gone back into the building. I thought of Teresa, the day she left her family. I finally knew how she felt.

CHAPTER TWENTY-SEVEN

AS IT TURNED OUT, LEAVING my job was a positive move. I still thought about Kathy every day but just knowing I wouldn't run into her helped me focus on my own life. I ended up getting a job selling life and health insurance and, though it was stressful in many ways, at least I didn't have to deal with the heavy issues I had to face everyday at the agency.

The training period was six months. All the new employees were assigned a mentor-- someone who had been with the company for at least five years whose main job was to teach the new people the ins and outs of selling insurance.

My mentor was a retired army man named Bill Willis. When I first met him, I wasn't sure I could stand being in the same room with him, let alone follow him around for six months. He looked like a "redneck" and talked like a tough guy. He called me "kid" and was proud that he voted for Barry Goldwater in the 1964 presidential election. My god, he was a Republican! But as I got to know him, I discovered that underneath his hard exterior, he was a real sweet guy. He took a liking to me and spent extra hours teaching me little "tricks of the trade".

I turned out to be quite successful, not so much because of my training with Bill, but because the compassionate listening skills I had developed as a social worker really helped me connect with people. Most potential customers trusted me instantly and easily opened up about their personal lives. Sometimes, I got so involved talking to them, they had to remind me why I was there. "Hey, weren't you going to talk to me about my insurance?" I'd laugh and say "Oh yeah." By that time, I didn't have to sell anything. I would just present a reasonable plan I knew they could afford. They usually said, "Okay. Write it up."

Bill was astonished. One day he took me aside. "I'll be real honest with you, kid. When you first walked through the door, I didn't think you'd last a month. Now look at you! Before long, you'll be training all of us old fogies. What's your secret?"

I laughed. "You know that I don't have a secret. I just talk to people and take an interest in them. They trust me."

Bill turned out to be right. Before long, the company promoted me to the position of sales manager.

I kept up my sessions with Gloria, only now I was just going once a week. I began to understand why I made the choices that I did and, in turn, better understood why the relationship with Kathy never could have worked. She pointed out to me that because I had so many losses in my life, it was difficult for me to make a real commitment. In fact, that may have been why Kathy was so attractive to me in the first place. Since I knew she couldn't totally commit to a gay relationship, she was safe. But during the course of the relationship, I started to heal. Kathy helped me immensely with that. When I got to the point of being ready for and wanting a total commitment, she couldn't give it to me. Even though I understood it better, I still felt really sad. Gloria said that would go away with time. I remembered telling Joey the same thing when his mother died.

I'd drop by Mary and Doug's house every now and then to see Joey. He was doing just great. He was elected president of his sixth-grade class and started getting interested in girls. Mary got pregnant soon after the adoption was final. When she called to tell me, she said, "You know, Susan, all of my friends told me that once we adopted a child, I'd be sure to get pregnant."

"It always seems to happen that way. I'm thrilled for you. I really am. How does Joey feel about it?"

"He can't wait. I really think he's old enough to share us with another child. My goodness, he's hardly ever here anymore. He's so popular and has so many friends."

When Jimmy turned one, Lynn and Dennis threw a birthday party for him. They invited all the little kids in the neighborhood, so Lynn asked if I would help organize things. She also asked if she should invite Kathy. She knew Jimmy would be happy to see her, but it was up to me. I felt guilty, but I said no. Jimmy had such a good time. He loved being the center of attention. I don't think he missed her at all.

I called Kathy occasionally. She told me she thought that she and Peter would be getting married shortly. At first, I felt hurt and jealous. But once I adjusted to the idea, I was sincerely happy for her.

"Are you really okay with this, Susan?"

"I think so. If it changes you'll be the first to know." But even as I said it, I really wondered if I could actually handle seeing her with someone else.

"I'm glad. I really want you in my life."

I made a lot of friends at work and my life on the outside was full. But I was still empty inside. I yearned for a close relationship, yet every time I had the opportunity to meet someone, I declined. I still felt too fragile to open myself up.

After about a year, my company offered me another promotion as the regional sales manager for the entire Southwest. "There's a catch, kid," Bill said. "You'll have to relocate to Phoenix. They want you there by the end of next week."

The hardest person to say goodbye to was Joey. I promised him that I'd write every month. "I know you have to go, Susan. I love Mary and Doug and I'm really happy here, but I'll still miss you."

"Joey, I'm going to miss you so much. You've been such a great friend. That's never going to end."

"Do you promise?"

"Yes, I promise. You don't have to worry. Remember the bird? I think you're strong enough to fly on your own."

"And you are too, aren't you Susan?" "Yeah, Joey. I am. I really am."

I met Kathy for lunch at the end of the pier. "Will you write to me, Susan?"

"How 'bout if I call. I'm not real good at writing."

"I feel I should say something really profound. This may be the last time I see you." I could see that she was holding back tears.

"Oh, I don't know about that. I have a feeling you'll always be in my life in some way."

"I hope you find someone wonderful to love you." "Like you have?" I really tried not to sound sarcastic. "Susan, don't."

"God, I don't know where that came from. I'm sorry. I really thought I was over all that. I guess I learn something new every time I'm with you."

"I guess some things are never over." She looked so sad. I had to force myself not to cheer her up.

"For you either?" I asked. "Yes, for me either."

We walked back to our cars in silence. There was nothing more to say.

CHAPTER TWENTY-EIGHT

I SPENT TWO YEARS IN PHOENIX. The one thing I remember most about it was the heat. In the summer, the temperature often got up to 118 degrees. There were days when I couldn't touch the door handle on my car without burning my fingers. And I couldn't get used to the landscaping in front of the homes and buildings. There was no grass! Just desert sand and what was called "Desert Flowers." Desert flowers weren't flowers at all. They were different kinds of cactus. The people in Phoenix thought they were beautiful. I thought they were ugly.

I lived in a one-bedroom apartment near my office in a nice part of town. It didn't matter much where I lived. I traveled so much that I was hardly ever there. My territory consisted of Arizona, New Mexico, Nevada and the western parts of Texas and Oklahoma. I wasn't in one place long enough to make any real friends but I did meet a lot of nice people that I enjoyed spending time with.

I kept my promise and wrote to Joey at least one time a month and called him on special occasions like Christmas and his birthday. His letters in my mailbox were always a welcome sight. He had a girlfriend now, named Molly. He joked that he liked her almost as much as he liked me. He sounded happy with his life, but usually ended his letters by asking when I was coming back. Besides Kathy, I missed Joey the most.

Lynn and Dennis had another baby -- a little girl they named Deborah. I promised Lynn that I would be there for her birth, but I was in Texas at the time and forgot to leave a forwarding phone number. By the time I got back, little Debbie was three days old. Lynn asked me to be her godmother. I told her I was flattered, but declined. I didn't know if I'd ever live in California again and I believed a godmother should be close by. She was hurt at first but finally agreed and reluctantly asked one of her other friends.

I called Kathy five or six times. She left the foster care agency and went into private practice. Her relationship with Peter ended abruptly when she found out he had been having an affair with his next-door neighbor. "He told me that it didn't mean anything, but can you imagine how I felt when I walked in on them?" Had she forgotten her old boyfriend in Kansas? I knew exactly how she felt.

Poor Kathy. She really deserved better. I wondered if she was getting sick of men lying to her. I wondered if she was attracted to men who couldn't commit. I wondered if she still thought about what we had together.

I told her that I was sorry it didn't work out, but I'm not sure I really meant it. As much as I denied it to myself, I think I was still hoping that she'd see the light and we would get back together someday.

I joined the National Organization for Women and went to meetings as often as I could. I met a very nice woman there. We'd go out for coffee after the meetings and talk about all kinds of things. I wasn't very political but she taught me a lot about women's rights and the gay women's movement. She was my first lesbian friend. Through her I started to understand how important it was to feel good about being a lesbian. She loaned me books written by gay women and took me to a gay pride parade. It was wonderful to read about women who had experienced the same feelings I had. It was like a 200-pound weight being lifted off my shoulders that I had carried around for much too long. I didn't feel so alone and isolated anymore.

Pat was a lot older than I was and had been in a happy relationship for twenty-one years. She and Donna, her partner, would invite me to parties at their home so that I could meet other single women. "You're much too wonderful to be alone, Susan. We're going to find you a lover if it's the last thing we ever do." They introduced me to several women that I went out with once or twice, but I couldn't stop comparing them to Kathy and nothing ever came of it.

One evening, I had just gotten out of the shower when the phone rang. It was Kathy. "Susan, I have some tragic news to tell you. Are you sitting down?"

"What is it?" I asked, thinking that her father died.

"Patsy was arrested. She caught Ed sexually molesting their ten-year-old daughter and she hit him over the head with a hammer. He's dead."

"Oh my God. I can't believe it."

"That's not even the worst part. She's quoted as saying 'I wasn't going to let him do this to another child of mine. He already did this to my oldest girl'."

"Kathy. Oh no, Teresa! I always knew there was something strange about them. I just could never believe they gave her up for the reasons they were claiming to."

"I know. You were right about that. I guess in a way, Patsy was trying to protect Teresa. But she got rid of the wrong person."

"Protecting her? It makes me sick---just the thought of him touching Teresa is horrible. He got what he deserved. But what about Teresa? Does she know? Why didn't she ever say anything?"

"When Betty told her, I guess she got hysterical. She had just blocked the whole thing out of her mind. She's been seeing a therapist and he advised Betty to take her down to the jail to see her mother. I heard it was quite an emotional scene. Patsy begged Teresa to forgive her. Poor Teresa. Betty told Mindy that the therapy is going along well, but it's going to take time for Teresa to heal. The therapist thinks that Teresa's emotional development stopped when the sexual abuse began. That's why she always seemed so young to all of us. Thank god you got her out of there, Susan. I shudder to think what might have happened to her if you didn't."

"How could Patsy have made those choices? She was so screwed up."

"Mindy thinks Patsy probably thought Teresa would never be safe, since she wasn't Ed's child. I guess he swore to her that if she would forgive him and let him stay, he would never touch his own children."

"Where are the other children?"

"They're in foster care. Actually, it's the only good thing to come out of this. Betty decided now that the adoption is final and Patsy's in jail, there's no threat Teresa will be taken away. So she's been taking Teresa over to see her brothers and sisters and now Teresa has a family again."

"That's wonderful of Betty to do that. I never got to know her well, but she sure turned out to be a blessing for Teresa."

"You were right about that too, Susan. She's been a terrific mom."

"You know. I kind of feel sorry for Patsy. It must have been a nightmare. What's going to happen to her?" I was genuinely concerned.

"I don't know. I suppose there'll be a trial."

"I wish I had pushed her harder in the beginning for a better reason to put Teresa in foster care. Maybe if I had, she would have broken down and told me the truth."

"You can't blame yourself for that. You did your best."

We were silent. Then she said, "Well, I thought you should know about it. How are you doing?"

"I'm fine. I think I might be moving back there in a few months. I'm really getting tired of all this traveling. I think I'd like to get back into Social Work."

"I'm glad. You're a great social worker. I should know." "So, I'll call you."

"Yes. Do that."

Eight months later, I ended up getting a job at a Family Service Agency in Orange County. Lynn had been sending me the employment section of the newspaper every week and I started sending out my resume. They flew me in for an interview and hired me on the spot. I got back just in time for Teresa's graduation from high school.

The auditorium was filled to capacity, so I just stood in the back. When Teresa marched in, I was able to catch her attention. "Hey, kiddo." She grinned from ear to ear when she saw me. She had been a lovely child. Now she was a beautiful young woman.

About halfway through the ceremony, someone hugged me from behind. I was startled and turned around with my fist clenched. "Don't hit me, Susan."

"Joey!" He was smiling widely. He had grown about five inches and was taller than I was. We stepped outside the door. "My god, you're all grown up!"

"Well, I am fifteen now."

"Oh, Joey. I'm so glad to see you."

"I think you'll be glad to see some other people too." He looked over my shoulder.

I turned around to see Mary and Doug. Doug was carrying a darling little girl. "Well, who do we have here?" I said, hugging them both.

"Susan," Mary said, "This is Susan."

Doug handed me the child. "Hi, Susie. You're a real cutie pie."

"It was my idea," Joey said proudly. "We all figured it's because of you that she's even here. We thought it was only fitting that we name her after you."

"I can't tell you how touched I am."

Mary looked inside. "I guess we missed most of the ceremony, huh."

"I think we can still see Teresa get her diploma."

We stood in the back and when Teresa's name was called, we clapped wildly. Some people turned around to look. It was then that I saw her. It had been over two years, and yet, it seemed like yesterday.

She smiled warmly when our eyes met. Then she turned around. "What is it, Susan? You're shaking."

"Nothing Joey. I'm just excited for Teresa."

When the graduates filed out, we went out to find her. She was standing with her brothers and sisters and, of course, Betty, who was proudly showing off her diploma. Teresa ran over when she saw us and grabbed my hand. "I'm so glad to see all of you. I didn't even know you were coming."

"Betty wanted it to be a surprise."

"It's the best present she could have given me. I love you all so much." Betty walked over grinning from ear to ear. She hugged Teresa. "Oh, honey, I'm so glad you like your surprise." And to me she said, "Thank you for coming. Thank you for everything."

I just nodded. I understood what she meant. I looked for Kathy. She was standing off to the side, watching us. I walked over to her. She looked tired. And she looked sad.

"You look beautiful, Susan. It's so good to see you." "I didn't expect to see you here."

"I came because Betty told me you might be here. I just wanted to see you again."

I smiled. "Well, here I am!" And then, "Kathy, what is it? Are you okay?" "Yes. I'm fine. Really."

I couldn't help myself. I hugged her tightly. She hesitated at first; then I felt her relax and hug me back. I didn't want to let go. "Why don't you come over and say hello to everyone?"

"I have to get going. I've already congratulated Teresa. You go ahead though."

"Come on, Kath. It will be fun. All of us being together again."

"No, Susan. Besides, this is your party. Look at them -- Teresa, Mary, Doug, Betty, Joey." Look how happy they all are. You did that, sweetheart. Without you, none of them would be here tonight."

"And without you, I wouldn't be here."

"You give me much more credit than I deserve. Now go. Have fun.

I have a lot of work to do."

"Will you call me soon?"

"I'm going to Kansas to see my folks in a few days. I'll call you when I get back."

"How are they, anyway?"

"Getting older. But hanging in there." "And Jenny?"

"She has a baby boy. She's very happy."

"Are you happy, Kathy? Are you seeing anyone?" "No. Go on, Susan. They're waiting for you."

"I love you, Kath. You're the best friend I ever had." Even though I had lost the battle, I still wanted her in my life.

"I feel the same way about you."

I turned and walked away. Then I looked back one more time. She smiled and waved. That was the last time I ever saw her.

It was wonderful to be with Joey and Teresa. They chattered back and forth in the restaurant like they were old friends. Mary let me hold Susie the whole time. I wondered if Kathy's sadness had to do with her not having a child. She always wanted one more than anything else.

I pulled Betty aside. "How's Teresa's therapy going?"

"It was difficult at first, but I think she's over the hump. She has a job for the summer as a camp counselor and then she'll be going away to college in the fall. Where did the time go?"

"Yeah, I know what you mean."

"Listen, I'm driving her up to camp on Saturday. Can I call you when I get back? Maybe we can go for coffee."

"I don't know Betty. I'm not even settled in yet." She paused. "You still love her, don't you?"

"I don't know. I haven't sorted it all out."

"I'd like to get to know you, Susan. It doesn't have to be anything heavy. I'm a real good listener."

"Thanks, Betty. I'll think about it."

Before I left, I made plans to take Joey to a Dodger game. I really needed something to look forward to.

"You're in luck, Susan," he joked. "My girlfriend is on vacation with her parents. I don't think she'd mind if I go out with an older woman."

"Well, I can't wait to meet her so that I can fill her in on what you were like when I first met you."

"You wouldn't do that, would you?"

"No. Not if you buy me a bag of peanuts at the game."

I hugged everyone goodbye and we all promised to get together soon. I felt really sad on the way home. Though I loved seeing them, it made me remember the times when they were such a big part of my life. The times I spent with Kathy. I couldn't stop thinking about her.

I called her the next day. "Kathy, I just wanted to tell you how great it was to see you yesterday."

"I enjoyed it too, Susan."

"You just looked so sad. Are you sure you're all right?" "Yes. I'm okay."

"You know, I've never regretted one minute I've ever spent with you." "What a lovely thing to say. That means a lot to me." She sounded distant. I probably shouldn't have called. "Well, have a good trip." "Thank you. And Susan..." "Yes."

"Just take care of yourself. And be happy."

I didn't hear from her again. She never told me she had breast cancer.

CHAPTER TWENTY-NINE

IT HAD BEEN SIX MONTHS since Kathy's death. I couldn't let it go. I kept having the same dream. I'd be walking into an airport terminal and I'd look at all the faces as I passed. I would see a woman standing in a ticket line with her back to me. My heart would stop as I got closer. I would call out "Kathy" and when the woman turned around, it was a stranger. I could feel my heart break.

I'd walk a little further down the terminal toward the last gate and all of sudden, there she was, walking toward me. We would both stop, in disbelief, and as I approached, I would see the tears begin to flow down her cheeks. When I got almost next to her I wouldn't be able to breathe. I would hesitate, but she'd smile, and open her arms. And in a second, I'd be in them, not caring who was watching or what people thought. I would feel her body from head to toe, but I could never get close enough.

"I can't believe you're here," I would whisper. "Please don't leave me again. I love you." And then, she would kiss me full on the lips and for that brief moment in time it was just the two of us, alone in an airport terminal as if no time passed at all.

"What do you think it means?" Gloria asked when I told her about it.

"I don't know. Isn't that your job?" She smiled. "Okay. Obviously, I didn't want her to die. I want her to come back."

"And if she did, what would you say to her?"

I started to cry. "I'd scream at her. Why didn't you take better care of yourself. This didn't have to happen. Why did you leave me without

197

saying goodbye?"

"Did you ever think that maybe death was her only way out?"
"What do you mean?"

"She was miserable with you; she was miserable without you. Maybe she just didn't want to be miserable anymore."

"I could have been there for her. I could have helped. It's like she died and left me with all the guilt."

"And doesn't that make you angry?"

"I wish I could get angry. Maybe I'd feel better."

"We'll work on that. But I think the dream is telling you something else." "What's that?"

"Susan, you're in an airport. I think she's telling you to let her go. Don't you think it's time to finally say goodbye?"

The plane touched down in Wichita right on schedule. I rented a car and went straight to the cemetery. As I drove in the gate, I began to cry. This would really make things final. I thought I was ready for it, but now I wasn't so sure. I got out of the car and counted the rows. The sixth row from the big oak tree, fourteen headstones down, the guard instructed.

When I got to the space, I looked down at the headstone:

Kathy Ann Adams
5/18/48 - 9/20/82
Beloved daughter of Don and Jessie
You'll be in our hearts forever

I put the flowers on her grave. I was crying so hard, I couldn't stand. I got on my knees and touched the stone lightly. I stayed with her for a long time. Finally, I said aloud," I have to say goodbye, Kathy. I will never forget you, my love. Thank you for sharing yourself with me. It was the most wonderful part of my life." I leaned over and kissed the stone, then turned and left.

I stopped for dinner before I went out to the house. I had to pull myself together. I had never met Kathy's mother, but I had talked to her on the phone briefly several times when she called. I also saw pictures of her that Kathy had shared with me and heard the many stories that she told about her family. I felt like I knew her.

As I walked up the driveway, she opened the door. "Come in, Susan. I'm glad to finally meet you. Kathy was so fond of you."

"I feel like I know you, Mrs. Adams. She talked so much about her family." "Did you get to the cemetery?"

"Yes." I started tearing up again. "I'm sorry. You don't need me bawling in front of you like this."

"I understand."

"I brought something for you. I thought you'd like to have some of the pictures I took of Kathy when we were...roommates." I handed her the album. She smiled as she looked lovingly through the pages. "She looks so happy. What a thoughtful thing for you to do." Then she was silent as she looked through them a second time.

"You know, Susan, one day, about a month before she died, I saw her crying in the living room. What is it, I asked. I thought she might be in a lot of pain. And then she told me about you."

"About me? What about me?" "She told me that she loved you."

"And I loved her too. She was a wonderful friend."

"No. I mean she told me everything." She touched my hand. "She was at peace with it and you should be too. I told her it's never wrong to love another human being. How could something so beautiful be wrong?"

"Oh, my God. Kathy must have been so relieved! She always worried that you wouldn't understand. I'm so glad that she finally told you." She put her arm around me as I cried. I kept thinking, thank God she didn't carry that guilt to her grave. When I finally gained my composure, I asked, "I have to know. Did she suffer?"

"I won't lie to you. Yes, she did. But after she was diagnosed with cancer, it was over pretty quickly. In the end, her family and friends were with her. She died peacefully in my arms. And we know she's with God."

"I wish I could have been there."

"She didn't want you to see her like that. She wanted you to remember her as she was. And she didn't want to put you through any more pain."

I broke down again. She brought me a tissue, and then gave me some privacy as I let everything sink in. When she came back she handed me a sealed envelope with my name on it. It was in Kathy's handwriting. "We found this in her things. I would have sent it to you, but I didn't know where you were, until now."

She had such a kind face. "May I hug you?" She held out her arms and hugged me warmly.

"Kathy wouldn't want you to be so sad. All she ever wanted was for you to be happy."

"I know. That's all I ever wanted for her too." She opened the album again and asked me about the pictures. I shared some of our happier moments with her and she shared some stories of Kathy's childhood with me. We knew that we were helping each other begin to heal.

When it was time to leave, I said, "I'd like to write to you once in a while." "I'd like that." I stood up and hugged her one more time.

"Well, goodbye and thank you again."

"Goodbye, Susan. You're a lovely young woman. I can see why Kathy loved you."

"It meant so much to me to be here. I won't forget you."

After the plane was in the air, I took the envelope out of my purse. I opened it slowly. The letter inside was dated September 3, 1976, the week before we moved in together.

Dear Susan,

There are so many things I want to share with you. I have this urgency to express my feelings as honestly as I can.

In the beginning, I was attracted to you because, well, first of all, you're beautiful. I don't believe I'd ever seen anyone as striking in beauty as you. And it grew from outward beauty to inner beauty. I loved what I saw, so real, so human, and so in need. You accepted me and in doing so began to make yourself vulnerable to me. I didn't have all the answers. I just responded to you. And you see, I always felt so inadequate. You were making me feel adequate. You have been the best friend I could have found. You've given me the chance to share my feelings openly with love. I want also to be an unbiased, non-judgmental friend for you. My love, the need for each other is overpowering. We must strive to strengthen the bond -- not to bind us but to set us free. You've opened my eyes. You've pointed out my self-worth and my need to be loved. Before I met you, I couldn't relax. I was feeling drained. You were there. You helped me relax. Your wit and humor are precious. You make me feel as if you had experienced my every feeling. Never knowing, yet always knowing. You knew my feelings of inadequacy, despair, unhappiness and pain. You never questioned. You always expressed a sensitivity and caring for my feelings being real. You truly are a beautiful person. I find comfort and security in loving and being loved by you.

I feel like a new-born child, innocent to self and others. I'm vulnerable to pain, but unlike the child, able to control my defenses. I feel strong and in control of my emotions, instead of them being in control of me. I truly see that in loving and choosing to love, I share in the plan for the world. And now I have you to help me carry out that task.

Love shared between us is a strength that has grown straight and strong, like a beautiful sunflower. And there on top is a gorgeous bloom, the seeds of which birds and the wind carry over the earth. The blossom is full and knowing its beauty, wants to be giving. But I must never forget my dependency on you. You are the water and sun and food I need for growth. You can restore and heal me if I admit my dependency on you and request your help. For I simply cannot go it alone.

For the first time in my life, the words life after death take on some meaning. For to you, I show myself and in doing so create a bond of love between us, that should I die tomorrow the love which we experienced will be passed on and go on living within others. Susan, you've freed me of the self-constraints I had bound myself with. You needed me to love you and I the same -- and what a reward. With you everything expressed is honest and true. The love I have found with you is a gift that I will cherish the rest of my life.

I love you.

Kathy

"Miss, are you all right?" I took his handkerchief and wiped the tears from my face.

"Thank you. I'm sorry I disturbed you. Yes, I'm fine."

As I folded the letter to put back in the envelope, I noticed the writing on the other side. It was dated September 8, 1982, just three weeks before she died.

Susan,

I found this letter among the things I treasure. I don't remember why I never gave it to you, but I want you to have it now.

Every word in it still rings true today. The days I spent with you were the happiest of my life. You really are the best friend I ever had. I'm so sorry that I disappointed and hurt you. You certainly deserved more. How I wish I could have been different. But I made the only choice I could have at the time.

Please don't be sad, my love. I have made my peace with God. I'm not afraid. I want you to be happy.

I want you to find someone to love who will love you back the way you deserve. It's time. You're such a wonderful person. I hope you know that by now.

Susan, I never, ever forgot our first kiss on the hill so long ago. My last thought on this earth will surely be of you.

I felt sorry for the man in the seat next to me. I cried all the way home. The next few months were very difficult, but with Gloria's help, I was able to understand that in order to find happiness in my life with someone else, I truly had to let Kathy go. The best way to honor her memory was to be that much freer person that she always encouraged me to be. Gloria pointed out that Kathy's pain was released through death; my pain was released through life. I realized that I was looking for someone just like Kathy to fill the emptiness I felt inside. Now I knew there would never be anyone just like her. But there could be someone I could love again. Just in a different way.

I was nervous as I dialed her number. "Hello, Betty. It's Susan. I'm sorry it's taken me so long to call, but I wanted to be sure. I'd really like to get to know you better too. If you'd like, I'm ready for that coffee now."

Printed in the USA
CPSIA information can be obtained
at www.ICGtesting.com
LVHW051019221024
794501LV00020B/453

9 781778 835018